power

Nicole Harman

one

In this world, people are naturally driven by one thing.

Power.

In the Royal community, the day you get your wings is the day you also gain your power. It's the very thing that defines a Royal. It sets you apart from others. It helps you discover who you are meant to be.

Unfortunately, there are individuals out there who find they aren't satisfied with the power that they have. They crave to have more. Then, there are people who discover that they have more power than they ever wanted.

I discovered I am one of these people. Someone who has more than they wanted. I am one of the individuals who possess more than one power; more than one ability.

Being a Mind Sight came with plenty of challenges as it was. However, I found out that this label was not entirely accurate. When a Royal has multiple powers, like me, they are what the Royal community calls a Mixer. I never wanted to be a Mixer. I never even wanted to be a Royal. All I wanted was my wings, to fit in.

Instead, I found myself to be this unique individual even in the Royal community. Many people were calling me lucky to have not one, but two powers, both of which, apparently, are rare. I didn't feel lucky. If I could, I would give it all up to have my best friend, my Hunter back.

Days became muddled together. I'm not sure how long it had been since the day Hunter died. Frankly, I didn't care. The seasons had changed, that much I did know. But, none of it seemed to interest me anymore.

At some point, I received a letter from home.

Mom had written to tell me about the memorial service they had back in Athra for Hunter.

Corbin was the one to deliver the news to Hunter's parents. I guess Agathin thought it best to send Corbin to tell them in person, being that he had some sort of relationship with them. Supposedly, they made Hunter's death sound heroic, saying that he had died saving a friend's life.

Not the full story, of course. But it was a need-to-know basis about being caught in an Exes attack, so they left that part out. I didn't even know about the memorial until after it happened. Had I known before it happened, I'm not even sure I would have attended. But I think I would have liked to have the option at least.

Each and every day, I could feel both of my powers growing inside of me. I want more than anything for them to stop. To go away. One of my powers made me see the moment that the attack happened and didn't allow me to stop it.

The other power almost drove me to kill a man. Something I didn't even know I was capable of until that day. I was terrified to use my abilities, finding myself only momentarily using my Sight to release the ache that the power tainted my body with.

I spent most of my time inside of my dorm. I didn't want to leave. I didn't want to learn any more about the powers that coursed through my veins. Part of me wanted to go home.

But as I began to realize, I didn't know where to call home anymore. I didn't belong in Athra. I didn't want to be the cause of anyone's death there. At least here in Banshui, there were plenty of people, plenty of Royals, with powers to defend themselves and others with. Though, without Hunter here, Banshui didn't feel like much of home either.

Since the day that Byrein came into my life, and Hunter left it, I felt a void of nothingness inside of my chest. A crushing sorrow that, most days, made it hard to breathe. Like a dark cloud of smoke surrounded me, embraced me at all times.

I found myself pushing everything and everyone away from me. I didn't know how to be around people, let alone feel anything other than this melancholy and dread. I just knew I didn't want to feel anymore. I didn't want to interact with others. This included Jewel, though she didn't quite care what I said to her or how I ignored her. She stayed, anyway.

"Good morning, Esmari!" Jewel sang as she walked gently into my dorm room. She didn't even knock anymore, partly because she didn't want me to tell her to go away anymore, I think. "It finally snowed last night. Did you see?"

"No," I said flatly.

"Oh, well, Banshui's first snow of the season is just as beautiful as ever. Come look!" Jewel invited, wrapping an arm around my shoulders and guiding me to the window. She pulled back the drapes and sighed as the bright daylight flooded into the room. "Fresh powder. Does it snow back in your Athra, Es?"

"No, not much," I told her. My voice was scratchy. *When was the last time I had a drink of water?*

Jewel seemed to notice too. She somehow never would make me feel bad for not doing basic things like showering or eating. She pulled out a juice from the fridge and cracked it open for me. She smiled softly as she played with the condensation that remained on her hands, stretching it like putty between her fingertips.

I hadn't seen her use her power in some time and had forgotten how foreign it looked. Her eyes caught mine and she smeared the water droplets from her fingers onto the pockets of her pants.

I took a sip of the juice, just enough to wet my throat. The flavors were less intense than they once were. Not sure if it was because I was becoming used to it, or because nothing seemed to taste the same since losing Hunter.

"Well, how about we go for a walk? There's just nothing like the feeling of the fresh Banshui snow under your boots," Jewel offered.

I looked down at my attire. I hadn't changed in days. My hair was still in the same messy bun it had been in since my last shower.

"I don't know," I said. The entire idea sounded like a lot more work than I was ready for.

"I'll wait for you to shower. Take your time," Jewel said, hanging gently on my shoulder while taking another look out the window at the glittering snow below. I took a deep sigh and nodded. She gave me a great big smile and asked, "Do you want me to get out some clothes for you, or do you want to pick them out?"

"Anything is fine, I guess."

"Okay," Jewel said. "I'll get you something out. I know what you have been liking to wear lately."

I wandered my way to the bathroom and Jewel turned on some low music. She hummed away to the tune of the radio as she began to rummage through my closet. I closed the bathroom door and took my shower. The warm steam was refreshing to my tired skin. I even found a new face scrub that Jewel must have snuck into my shower for me to use.

When I was all clean and dry, I changed into the clothing that Jewel had picked out for me. Black pants, a dark gray sweatshirt, and some lace-up boots with fir lining. Jewel sat by my window and waited for me. Not once did she bother me about how long I was probably taking.

When I had dressed, Jewel placed my dirty clothes into my overflowing hamper and grabbed out the hairdryer. She sat me down in a chair and dried and styled my dull blonde hair, all the while continuing to hum away with the radio's music.

At some point, my emotions got the best of me and tears began streaming down my face for a moment. Jewel dropped the brush in her hands on the ground and wiped the tears from my cheeks. She held me for that moment, without a word, until the tears stopped. Then, she picked up the brush and finished my hair as if nothing even happened.

After locking up our dorm rooms, we headed down the tile stairs and out the door of our dorm building. I couldn't remember the last time I had stepped foot outside of the building, and I found myself anxious to do so. Jewel gave me a quick smile and linked arms with me, just as she had always done. Gently, she tugged at me, urging me to take my first step into the bright white snow.

The crunch from under our feet made her giggle with glee. She released my arm and took a big jump into an ankle-deep mound of snow. Her iridescent wings flittered on her back as she laughed. Again, she jumped, like a little kid. She flashed me a smile and gathered up a snowball in her bare hands.

"Please, don't," I begged Jewel, growing nervous over whether she was about to throw it in my direction.

"I'm not going to throw it at you, silly!" she exclaimed, handing me the ball of snow. "You're going to throw it at anything you want!"

I looked at her, feeling ridiculous. She nodded at me, prompting me to fulfill her wish. Finally, she took a handful of her own and chucked it at the trunk of a nearby tree. It slammed against the bark and exploded with a thud. I tossed it at the tree as well, watching the chunks of snow rain down after impact.

"Now you know what it feels like to have a power like mine!" Jewel laughed. "Well, kind of. It's a bit less cold generally."

I shook my head with an almost-smile and she handed me another snowball. We began aiming for limbs on the tree, trying to see who would hit it first, or make the biggest snowball explosion, until my hands began to grow numb from the cold. Shoving our hands deep into our sweatshirt pockets, we rested for a moment and just listened to the sounds of the world around us. My arms started to ache, but I knew it wasn't just from the cold.

"Look who has finally left her room!" rang an all too familiar, high-pitched excuse of a voice. Belleza strode over toward us, with Lilly at her heels, as always. "Lilly, don't get too close, some of her gloom will rub off on you."

"Lezzy, we had better watch out!" Lilly laughed along. Raising a dainty, pink, manicured hand to her lips, she gave a fake gasp.

"Aren't these dorm rooms for students? From what I hear, you haven't been studying lately. When was the last time you even stepped foot in the academy?" Belleza smirked as she toyed with a strand of her long brown hair, delicately draped over one shoulder.

I clenched my jaw shut. Anger rose within me. I could feel the ache in my shoulders growing stronger. I wasn't sure which power was nagging at me, but I certainly didn't want to find out in front of Belleza. My breath caught in my throat as she let out one of her hair-raising cackles.

The urge to release my power grew stronger. All I could think about was getting out of there. I turned quickly and headed for the door. Jewel snapped some quick remark toward Belleza, but I was too heated to listen to what it was.

Throwing open the door, I stormed inside and raced up the stairs. I could hear Jewel's wet boots squeaking against the tile flooring just behind me.

"Es!" she called.

I didn't turn back. I couldn't turn back. The

ache grew stronger and stronger. My hands were sweating as I balled them into fists, digging my nails into my palms.

I wanted to be alone. Away from anyone. It was becoming increasingly apparent that this was not my Sight. It was my other power, the one I still didn't know the name of. The one that could hurt people.

I wanted to throw up. I had spent so long suppressing this power. *Why now? Why here?*

"Es, come on," Jewel pleaded with me.

Please, Jewel. Leave me alone. I didn't know how to form the words in my mouth. My jaw was locked shut now as I tried to keep my power inside. It had been hours since I had used my Sight. *Was that why? Was it too much for my body to keep inside any longer?* I rounded the corner and slammed straight into someone. Belleza's cackle echoed in my head again as I fell to the ground. My veins burned.

"Ah!" I growled.

A surge of power released from me without warning or permission. It was like a wave of multicolored electricity pushing out away from me, with me as its center; the sound of static echoing with.

A moment later, I felt a release of pressure. I sat on the floor panting, trying to catch my breath. Looking around, fear washed over me. Jewel sat just feet behind me, rubbing at her head. In front of me, Kasius sat on the ground and stared right at me with his face of stone.

I didn't know what to do or say. I didn't know how to apologize. I looked at my hands that were blotchy from the cold and use of power. I was embarrassed, terrified of my own abilities. Terrified of my lack of control. *How could Jewel trust me now? How could I trust myself?* The idea of it made me want to scream and hide all at once.

I chose to hide. Standing up, I ran directly for my dorm and slammed the door shut behind me.

"Esmari!" Jewel's still-shaking voice beckoned from outside.

"Go away!" I pleaded.

I collapsed on the middle of my floor, trembling tears trickling down my face. I hugged my legs hoping to feel some sort of security. I squished my knees into my body. I wanted so badly to fill in the gaping hole in my chest.

"Es, come on," Jewel said, her voice muffled

from behind my door. "Are you okay?"

Am I okay? How could she be asking if I was okay? I just sent her into the ground! Anger built up inside me once more. *How could you do this to her! How could you be such a monster, Esmari!*

"Es, you didn't do it on purpose. It's okay," Jewel said, cautiously opening the door.

"Please, Jewel. I don't want to hurt you. Please leave me alone," I sobbed.

"No, you need to get the urge of your power out. I can guarantee that didn't fulfill it. Am I right?" She walked softly into the room and snagged a half-full water bottle from beside the bed. She sat next to me and poured some into her hands. "Let's play that game, the one where you tell me the shape that I'm making with the water using your Mind Sight. Surely, that will help ease the tension in your shoulders."

I looked up at my friend's smiling face. She wasn't the least bit angry. A blonde strand of her now tangled, orange-tipped hair flopped to the wrong side of her part. I caught a glimpse of movement from behind her.

Kasius stood calmly, watching us in my doorway. His eyes were soft as he nodded at me.

"Okay," I finally agreed.

"Alright!" Jewels exclaimed. I think she enjoyed this game more than I did anymore. But she was right. It did help to silence my urges. "What shape?"

With the sleeve of my sweatshirt, I smeared the tears from my face. I pressed my fingertips lightly against the ground and closed my eyes, taking a moment to calm my emotions. A jolt of power later and I could clearly see Jewel smiling away, with her hands forming the water in front of her.

"A horse," I smiled.

"Wow, that was quick. You are getting better!" Jewel beamed.

"So are you." I smirked. "That one actually looked like a horse this time."

"Hey!" Jewel scoffed with a laugh. "Let's see you try then!"

My short-lasting smile turned quickly into unease and discomfort again. Guilt was eating me apart from the inside. I looked once again at my hands as the memory from the hall flashed in my head. Jewel laying on the ground. She looked just like the man that killed Hunter the way she was. *What if I had accidentally injured her? Killed her even?* I shuddered at the thought. Jewel glanced up at the clock on my wall with her wide blue eyes and took a sigh.

"I have class in a little bit here," Jewel mentioned. "Are you coming with me to the academy today?"

"Jewel—" I started.

"You don't have to go to your class. If you want to come with me to mine today, you can. I could show you around finally, and maybe show you what I am working on. It's just a scheduled lab time. Belleza and Lilly already had theirs, so they surely won't be there." Jewel rambled trying to convince me. I hadn't stepped foot in the academy since I discovered I was a Mixer.

"No, I'm not ready for that," I said, looking down.

Reality was, the very thought of going back made my stomach turn in knots. I wasn't ready to face who I was becoming, and going to the academy would force me to do so. I have no idea who would teach me. I wasn't ready for the way that everyone would look at me.

Jewel stood and took a brief sigh. "Okay," she

said. "When you're ready."

I nodded a silent thank you to her. She looked at me with sorrow in her eyes, hesitant to leave. Kasius finally stepped into the room. He nodded for Jewel to take her leave. She gathered her things and headed out the door.

Kasius and I paused in the silence for a moment. His one hand was tucked just inside of the pocket on his slacks. His tucked-in, gray button-down shirt sat neatly on his shoulders.

"Come. You need to eat," he said, offering out a hand to help me up.

I hesitated. My breath caught in my throat. "No, I'm okay," I said. Feeling uncomfortable, I looked down at the ground.

Kasius came over to where I was sitting on the floor. He crouched down and took a hand to tilt my chin. His eyes met mine. I took in his striking features for a moment. The burgundy in his hair was less noticeable in the lack of light in my room.

"It wasn't a question," he stated plainly. He stood and offered a hand again, in such a way that I didn't deny it once more.

I followed him down the hall to the kitchen area where he sat me down at one of the seats of the counter and headed to his dorm to retrieve some food. A few moments later, he returned and began to prepare the food. I felt awkward with him doting on me. I didn't deserve for him to be nice to me. *I basically just attacked you in the hallway. I haven't talked to you for I don't even know how long. You should be mad at me, not kind.*

Kasius placed a bowl of salad and a half of a sandwich in front of me. I could feel his gaze as I stared down at the food before me. From the corner of my eye, I saw his lips curl into the smallest smile before he took a bite of his salad. I took a timid bite of food as well.

"You've been avoiding me," he stated. It wasn't a question.

"Yeah, well," I sighed. "I haven't really talked to anyone."

"Except Jewel," he noted.

"Yeah," I mumbled.

"Esmari," he said, his voice smooth and calm, "I'm not upset at you."

"You should be. I just attacked you," I scoffed under my breath.

"No, not from where I was standing. You didn't," Kasius said.

"I sent both you and Jewel to the ground. I did that," I said gritting my teeth.

He shrugged. "Not on purpose."

My fingers began to tingle again, prompting me to use my Sight again. *I just used Sight, why am I feeling this way again?* I ignored it, pushing the feeling out of my mind. I turned to face Kasius as he finished up his sandwich.

"Shouldn't you be at the academy?" I asked. It wasn't like him to miss classes.

"Shouldn't you?" He smirked.

"I don't belong there. You do. I sincerely hope you aren't missing class just because of me." Agitation and guilt pressed against my chest like a heavy weight.

The urge of my power was now spreading its way up my arms and pinching at the nape of my neck. I pushed my plate away and balled up my fists, scrunching my eyes shut. *Go away! I don't want to use my power. Please. Go away.* I felt a hand on my shoulder and I opened my eyes.

"Which one?" he asked.

"Sight."

"One thing I do know about our abilities is that you can't stop them. It's not safe to hold them in."

"In my case, it's not safe to use them either," I said, knowing very well that he was right.

I shook my head and felt a strong pulling into my shoulders. With a sigh, I knelt against the ground, allowing the tips of my black, uneven wings to brush against the floor. I glanced up at Kasius, who was watching me patiently, and took a deep breath. *Now's as good a time as any.* Another twinge rippled through my arms, up to the nape of my neck. Reluctantly, I touched the ground and closed my eyes. *Go ahead, show me what it is that is so important.*

I waited a moment and then felt all of my surroundings slipping away. I could see a figure. A man. He was being pinned to the ground by a person wearing an ORP jacket. I focused in on his gaunt face. *He's the one who attacked Hunter. The one who attacked his home.* I could see his face clearly. He wasn't upset. He was smiling, even.

A voice echoed in my ears. "A gift," it said.

It was Byrein's voice. I was sure of it. I looked for a moment longer at the man's face, his eyes, they seemed soulless. Not like the way they did the last time I saw them. Then all of my surroundings came back to me.

A buzzing in my ear made me realize I had gone unconscious again this time. I swallowed hard and shook my groggy head. I reached for the dainty charm of my necklace, rubbing against the faint, crack-like veins of the black stone in my fingertips.

I hadn't seen or heard anything about Exes for such a long time. Now, this. *Why today?* The fact that Byrein was now capable of speaking to me during my Sight episodes unnerved me, making my skin crawl at the very idea. I didn't understand how he was capable of it. *Am I capable of this, too?* I shook the thought from my head. I didn't want to be capable of this.

"Esmari?" Kasius cooed.

I had entirely forgotten he was there. I looked at him for a moment, considering what to say. I didn't want to tell him about it. I didn't want to think about it anymore. I just wanted to pretend it didn't happen. I wanted it all to just go away.

"I want to be alone," I said finally, standing to my feet. Kasius sighed quietly but didn't object. I went straight back to my dorm and shut the door behind me.

two

I woke the next morning to a tapping on my door. It was a bit on the early side, as the sun was just beginning to seep into my room from a crack in my curtains. I rolled over in bed, still wrapped up in my sweatshirt from the day before.

A flood of thoughts from the events of the day before rushed through my mind. I moaned and shoved my face into my pillow as if to stifle them out. It didn't work.

The door squeaked open. "Good morning, Es," Jewel said treading lightly into my room.

"Go away, please," I mumbled. "Let me sleep."

"Es, someone is downstairs for you," Jewel continued. For a moment her voice and presence reminded me of my mom.

"I don't want to see anyone."

"It's Mr. Sean. I can't just tell him to go away. I don't think he'd listen, even if I tried," Jewel said.

I took a sigh and sat up. "What does he want?" I asked, confused.

Jewel shrugged. "I'm not sure. To talk to you, I guess."

"Fine," I scoffed.

I tossed my tangled hair into a messy bun and slid into some shoes. Jewel linked her arm with mine, flashing me a smile filled with enough confidence for the both of us, then we headed downstairs.

Mr. Sean stood hunched in the slightly crowded lobby of the dorm, looking completely out of place. His hands were shoved deep in trench coat pockets, and he wore a scowl on his scruffy, bearded face. Momentarily, he brought a hand up to the bridge of his nose and gave it a pinch. It was almost comforting to see how much he hadn't changed.

"It's been a while," Mr. Sean stated in his raspy tone.

I raised my eyebrows and nodded. "Yup," I breathed.

Mr. Sean looked around at the room, growing increasingly more crowded with students preparing for their day, and I could tell that his Sight power was making it uncomfortable for him to stay much longer. "Let's talk outside," he offered.

Jewel and I followed him to a nearby picnic bench, which was surprisingly dry from yesterday's snowfall. We took a seat across from Mr. Sean who grunted as he settled down.

I found it hard to look at him and instead stared at the cracking paint on the wood of the table. A brisk breeze toyed with a stray piece of hair on my neck.

"Well, I'll get right to the point," Mr. Sean said. "I thought you would like to know that they caught the Ex who caused Hunter's death."

"I know," I said plainly.

"I guess he didn't even put up a fight. Like he

couldn't. Almost like he turned himself in," Mr. Sean's voice trailed for a moment. "Wait, what do you mean you know?"

Jewel now glanced over at me with a mix of confusion and concern on her face. I lifted a hand and tapped a finger to my temple, looking at Mr. Sean. "Mind Sight, remember?"

"You saw," he said with a sigh.

"Why didn't you say anything?" Jewel asked.

I looked away. Byrein's words echoed in my memories. I swallowed hard, growing agitated. I shoved my hands in the pouch pocket of my sweatshirt and looked at the muddy snow around us. It surprised me how the snow still remained on the ground, but the air didn't feel cold enough for it to stick around.

"If that's all you wanted," I said, beginning to stand.

"Esmari, when are you goin' to start your studies again? You can't just hide away forever," Mr. Sean said sternly.

I turned and looked him dead on. I could feel my ears getting hot with irritation. "Why do you care?"

"You haven't figured out how to control it,

have you? You don't always choose what to see. You have to see what your power is allowin' you to see. You can feel it growin' stronger inside of you by the day, am I right? You have got to learn how to control it," Mr. Sean said, standing to his feet, agitation laced in his gravelly voice.

"Who are you to tell me what to do? You have no right!" I snapped.

"It's consuming you. And, if you don't figure out how to take control of it, it will control you. You know this more than anyone. I'm sure it's already gettin' to that point! I know, I can see it written all over your face!" Mr. Sean continued.

"Es, what does he mean?" Jewel said with concern.

"So, what if it does! You dropped me off in Mr. Higgens' office the second you figured out what I was!" I hissed at Mr. Sean. I could feel my wings twitching with agitation on my back.

Mr. Sean clenched his jaw for a moment. "I'll teach you," Mr. Sean said finally. It was as if the words were poison to his lips.

"Now you'll teach me?" I scoffed, narrowing my eyes at him. "Is this a joke?"

"No, I'll teach you. If that's what it will take for

you to come back. I'll take you as a student again," Mr. Sean said. Based on the tone in his voice, I could tell he hadn't thought the idea through completely.

"So, what, I'm just supposed to go crawling back to you? After everything that happened?" I sneered. There was a twinge in my wings and my hands were tingling with anger. "Learning now is not going to bring Hunter back."

"Neither is ignoring your power, hopin' it will go away!" Mr. Sean snapped back.

He was right. I hated that he was right. "How are you even supposed to teach me? You aren't a Mind Sight. Let alone whatever else I am!" My heart was pounding in my ears as I spoke.

"I don't know. But you and I both know that continuin' to suppress either of your powers isn't good. It's not safe. The more you do so, the more dangerous you are. You are goin' to hurt someone or even yourself," Mr. Sean said frankly.

"Es, what is he talking about?" Jewel said.

I clenched my jaw and dug my nails into my palms. I felt lost. I trembled with anger. I didn't want to learn my power. I wanted my power to disappear. Quite frankly, *I* wanted to disappear. I could feel a burning sensation racing through my arms down to my fingertips. I squeezed my eyes shut, trying to stop the tears of frustration from coming down my face. *What does he know? I asked him to teach me so many times. But he refused! And now he will teach me? I'm not even sure I want him to teach me!*

"Esmari," Mr. Sean said, startling me out of my thoughts. "Look at your hands."

I looked down at my fists, balled up at my sides. There was a glow around them of swirling power, alternating with hints of different colors. It was like a mist, sparking every so often with flickers of something that reminded me of electricity. My breath caught in my throat as I took a gasp. I looked up and saw Jewel taking a couple of steps back, distancing herself from whatever I was going to do.

"Esmari, just calm yourself down." Mr. Sean stood directly in front of me. He wasn't scared like Jewel was. He was firm, unwavering. His sudden sense of respectable authority caught me off guard and made me feel even more vulnerable than usual.

I took a shaky breath in and calmed my

emotions. The burning in my hands stopped, as well as my arms. I let my tears overflow my eyes and trickle down my cheeks, cooling my face with the winter breeze. Tiny snowflakes began to fall around us from the gray skies above. I looked Mr. Sean in the eyes and swallowed hard as the last bit of glowing power faded from my hands.

Mr. Sean nodded slowly. "Tomorrow, nine o'clock," Mr. Sean instructed, then he turned abruptly and strode away.

———

Jewel walked with me to the academy the next morning. I felt more nervous than I expected, realizing I was going to have to face my powers. Not only face them, but use them, learn them, control them even. The very idea made my stomach do flips.

We stood at the doors for a moment. A brisk shiver from the morning breeze raced down my spine, and I decided it was time to face what the day had in store for me.

When we entered the towering double doors into the lobby of the academy, my nostrils were met with the familiar scent that its walls held. It brought a sense of comfort to my anxious nerves, surprisingly. There was a bit more of a bustle about the academy this morning, more than I remembered for this early in the morning. *Okay, Es, you can do this.*

"You going to be okay?" Jewel asked cautiously flashing me a gentle smile.

I nodded, though I wasn't quite sure myself. She waved me goodbye and was on her way to her own class, soon after, leaving me standing in the lobby. For a moment longer, I lingered, glancing once again at the charcoal gray script letters painted on the taupe wall just above the staircase.

"Professor Javion's Academy for Royalty," I read to myself in a whisper, then took a sigh and shoved my hands into my frumpy sweatshirt pocket.

I mustered up the courage to take the necessary steps, leading myself down the winding hallways to the Sight classroom in the back depths of the academy. My sneakers squeaked against the tile flooring as I walked through the halls, which were growing dimmer and dimmer the further I got from the main lobby. It was quiet, as usual, back here, which somehow made me feel a bit more secure.

The clock on the wall showed two minutes to nine when I entered the single black door to the classroom. Mr. Sean was waiting for me in the center of the brick flooring, his hands tucked away in the pockets of his trench coat. He took a look at me and sighed.

"I almost didn't think you would come," he said coldly.

I swallowed hard and looked at the dust on the ground, around my shoes. Biting my tongue, I suppressed the snarky comment hindering in my throat. I was too tired to argue with him today, let alone with myself.

A flood of emotions made my heart pound in my chest, remembering the last time I had stepped in this room. An image of Hunter in the rubble crept out of my memories. I didn't like it here.

"Mr. Higgens has requested to see you first thing this mornin'," Mr. Sean croaked finally.

Without another word, he walked out the door, only pausing for a moment to wave for me with a calloused hand to follow. I took a breath and went with him, not feeling like I had much of a choice anyway.

We wound through the halls of the academy, back out to the lobby, where we passed by students exchanging whispers and flicking looks my way. My eyes met Belleza's for a moment. She gave one of her smirks, eyeing me as we began to ascend the stairs. I glared back just long enough to make her uncomfortable, before turning and continuing on my way.

At the top of the staircase, we veered down the hallway, heading toward the bright red door at the very end. Mr. Sean gave Mr. Higgens' office door a solid knock. Not waiting for an answer, he entered. Mr. Higgens nodded hello and waved for us to take a seat as he finished his phone call.

"—yes—thank you—we will talk soon," he said with his rich, deep voice, then returned the phone to its base and quickly ran a dark-skinned hand over his curly gray-haired head. "Good morning, Esmari, Mr. Sean."

"Morning," I said reluctantly. *We will see if it turns out to be a good one or not.*

I took in a breath of the sweet cinnamon scent lingering in the air around us as I settled back into the large, black leather armchairs. A pause of uncomfortable silence engulfed us, and I found myself glancing at the multitude of dainty sculptures that were strategically placed on his chock-full bookcase. *There are more of those than I remember.*

"It's good to see you back within the walls of the academy, Esmari. I understand you have reservations upon returning, in light of all that you have been through," Mr. Higgens said softly as he stood, pushing his chair from the dark wooden desk. He took his intricately carved cane and made his way to the bookshelf at the side of the room. He leaned his back against it and peered in my direction with his dark brown eyes, hoping for a response. I offered him none. He took a breath and continued. "Mr. Sean tells me that he has taken you as a student once again, and you have accepted."

"Yes, for the time being," I stated plainly.

"Good. I look forward to hearing of your progress with your Mind Sight. As for your other power. This is a bit more, well, tricky." Mr. Higgens paused and scratched at his brow. "I did not see your power happen, but Mr. Sean did see part of it. I have spoken with Agathin and we have some theories, but nothing concrete as to what this other power of yours is. Truly, we haven't heard of anyone in Banshui with something similar."

My ears perked. "What about elsewhere? Is there someone else from some other area? Some other Royal community?" I blurted out.

"I should rephrase. We don't *currently* have anyone with this power. However, there are records that make us wonder if you have a long-lost power. Something that didn't get passed down in the more recent generations." He pondered as he spoke.

"So, what you're telling me is that you don't know what I am," I sighed, feeling defeated.

"We know you are a Mixer. Someone with more than one power or ability. That much is certain. However, it tends to be difficult with Mixers. Especially when a Mixer has two rather rare abilities. It becomes difficult to discern where one classification of ability ends and the next one starts. Sometimes it's hard to tell which ability you might be using at a certain time; you quite possibly could be using both together. Which of course is not necessarily a bad thing, just can make classification and initial steps of learning a bit tricky," Mr. Higgens explained.

"Higgens, have you seen anythin' like this power before?" Mr. Sean spoke up.

Mr. Higgens paused for a moment and looked at the two of us, then nodded gently. "Yes, when I was very little, I remember a single man here in Banshui who had something similar. Though, it was so many years ago, that I don't know just how similar it was to yours. But that's what made me research into this side of things. The long-lost powers, that is."

"Do you know what they called it?" I asked, feeling for the first time like I was finally getting some answers.

"I remember it was something along the lines of an Energy power. Again, I didn't know the man well, and I was very young when he passed." Mr. Higgens looked at me with apologetic eyes. "From the records that Agathin had on him, he never had any children. He was, however, like you, without Royal parents, but they were both residents of Banshui. Esmari, I know this is not very useful of information to you. I'm sorry, child."

I shook my head. "It's better than nothing."

"Esmari, I want you to understand that, while we cannot provide you with a teacher to help you with this Energy power, if that is the correct name for it, we want you to feel safe and welcome to learn this ability. And if I, or Mr. Sean, can assist, we will."

I began to feel a tingle in my fingertips. I hadn't used either of my abilities all morning. Quickly, the sensation moved up my arms and into my shoulders. I shifted uncomfortably in my chair.

Mr. Higgens eyed Mr. Sean as if exchanging a silent conversation. I was pretty sure it was my Sight, but I didn't want to be wrong. Not near people. Not inside of the Head of the Academy's office. *Just ignore it, Es. You'll be out of here soon, and then you will use it.*

"Esmari?" Mr. Higgens questioned.

The urge was becoming more uncomfortable by the second. I swallowed hard and took a deep breath. Quickly, I noted my surroundings. I lifted one hand to my necklace and felt it between my fingertips, focusing on each of the tiny grooves on the stone. I glanced at Mr. Sean and Mr. Higgens, hoping that we would be done with the meeting soon.

"Esmari, are you alright?" Mr. Higgens asked.

"Holdin' it in won't help. You know that," Mr.

Sean said plainly.

He was right. It wasn't helping to hold it in. I glanced around again at the office. It felt small and crowded. *Just go into the hallway, Es.*

"Can you excuse me for a moment?" I asked, already getting up. I didn't wait for an answer.

I tossed open the door and stepped into the hallway. Thankful that it was empty, I knelt down, pressed a palm into the ground, and closed my eyes.

A surge left my hand. The Ex who attacked Hunter appeared. He sat there, just staring. He was sitting at a table in an empty room, just staring directly forward into the space before him.

I kept looking at his face. There was something different about his eyes. It wasn't the appearance, per se. But it was almost like the spark was gone. Like a part of him was missing, somehow. They were soulless and cold. Though he didn't seem upset about it.

A person with ORP on their sleeve finally came into the room. The Ex didn't move. He looked content.

My surrounding sounds returned to my ears. I grunted as I stood up. My shoulders hurt, as well as my neck. I rubbed at my half-asleep knees and placed a hand on my necklace to remind myself that the Sight episode was over.

Looking up, I saw a still, quiet hallway, though I felt off in a way. As I turned around, I saw Mr. Sean leaning in the doorway, hands in his coat pockets, Mr. Higgens just behind.

Were they watching the whole time? I thought back, realizing I hadn't shut the door after I left the office. *Good job, Es.* I took a sigh and looked down, feeling exposed and uncomfortable, not really sure what to say to the both of them. At least the sensation in my arms and hands had stopped.

Mr. Sean sighed and I looked up to see him open his mouth, only to close it and consider his words. He pinched at the bridge of his nose for a moment and then looked at me again. "You were there a while," he finally said.

Odd comment to have. I shrugged. "Okay." I tucked my necklace under the collar of my sweatshirt and stuffed my hands into the pouch pocket. The soft, fuzzy inside was relaxing against my hands.

"You don't realize how much time you've lost, do you?" Mr. Sean said coldly.

Had I been there long? I looked at him and shrugged again. "So?"

"Esmari, you were there over a half-hour," chimed Mr. Higgens.

I swallowed hard. *Thirty minutes? How could that be? That wasn't right, was it?* My mind raced over the time loss. There was a pressure about Mr. Sean's presence, one that I couldn't understand. I could feel my palms begin to sweat. My wings twitched on my back. *Just calm down, Es. It's fine. So, you had been there for a while? No big deal, right?*

I took a shaky breath in and slowed my mind. Looking down at my sweatshirt, I could see a mild glow from my pocket where my hands were. *Not now, not here.* Anxiety and fear grew inside my chest.

Mr. Sean saw as well, but he didn't ask me to calm down this time. He just watched for a moment, and then nodded to Mr. Higgens to see as well. I felt like I was some kind of show for them.

"Take your hands out of your pockets," Mr. Sean instructed.

I could feel my ears growing hot with embarrassment. I didn't want to show off my now-glowing hands. I wanted them to stop glowing.

Another moment passed, and I could see my fear was not helping. It was making them brighter.

I slowly slid my hands out of their hiding spot. Near my fingertips, which were scrunched deep into my glowing, bright-white palms, were faded colors, rotating through blue, to purple, to pink, and so on. I saw Mr. Higgens' eyes widen at the sight of them with a look of intrigue. Gradually, it faded away, leaving my hands bare and normal.

Mr. Higgens scratched at his scruff on his chin. "I think until you get control of this power of yours, it may be best for you to have a separate room; a space that is just your own to go to, that you won't worry about others inside, or anything that you might damage. Somewhere, that you can explore this power of yours, safely."

It was the best thing he had said all day. I nodded with a sense of relief washing over me for the first time in months.

three

I fell back into routine easier than I had expected to. Though, part of me felt like I was going about my day just as mindless as before, except I was no longer in my own dorm room.

By the end of the week, Mr. Higgens and Mr. Sean had set up a room for me to essentially "escape" to when I felt my other power that we nicknamed my Energy, until we could figure out just what it was. The room, my Energy safe room, was just two doors down from my other classroom, to allow for my access as needed. I was grateful for it all being in the back, hidden corner of the academy. Secluded, and out of sight.

Mr. Sean helped ease me back into the learning process. I found his patience with me very out of character for the first day or two, but that quickly faded, and he turned back into the inpatient grump that I was used to.

"Here, try this today," he grunted at me as he tapped at the open page of the book now resting on the podium.

"Yeah, okay," I said under my breath. I tucked a stray strand of hair behind my ear and took a sigh. While I was getting used to being here, a part of me still really wanted to be back in my dorm, alone.

Mr. Sean paused and looked me over for a moment. Turning away, he headed toward his office. "Watch your time. Lunch is at noon," he called over his shoulder, pointing up toward the clock.

He entered his office, leaving the door cracked. It was like he read my mind, and I was grateful. I wasn't in the mood today to be around him, or anyone else for that matter. However, I knew that he left the door cracked so he could still keep an eye on me, which, though I didn't want to admit it aloud, I didn't mind too much.

For a moment, I stared at the book, not reading. I zoned out, just thinking about nothing. It had been a long week, and I was beginning to realize how tiring it had been.

A memory of Hunter's smiling face popped into my head. It made me feel warm and also empty inside all at once. I took a breath and held on to the memory for a second more. *Hunter, how I wish you were here. I'm sure you would get on me for slacking in my studies.* I smirked to myself at the thought and began reading through the chapter.

By noon, I had just made it through the history and explanations of the reasons for the Mind Sight exercise. I decided to leave off there, saving the instructions for the afternoon. My arms were tingling once again, though less intense today than normal.

I knelt down and pressed a couple of fingers to the ground. Instantly, a small, shock-like surge left my fingers. I saw students entering the cafeteria. A teacher nodded to a few students as he left.

When my surroundings came back, I glanced at the clock, something I found myself doing each time I had an episode now. Twelve o' five. *Didn't lose much time, this time.* I stood and pulled the sleeves of my loose black sweater over my cool hands, then headed toward the cafeteria for my lunch.

Jewel was waiting just inside the door for me. She looked chipper as ever when she caught sight of me, almost skipping over to link arms with me. Jewel brushed a strand of hair out of her face with the back of her hand. She and I made our way to our usual line to gather up our lunch and found a seat at an empty table.

"Have I told you how great it is that you are back at the academy again? Because, it is really, really great. It was such a lonely few months eating without you, you know," Jewel rambled as she stirred her steaming soup. I pushed my vegetables around on my plate with a fork, realizing I was not very hungry. "So, how's it going anyway? Are you making any progress with your Mind Sight? Or what about your other power?"

I turned to glance at her. Giving her a quick shrug, I frowned and turned back to my plate. I wanted to answer her but didn't feel like I had the energy, let alone any answers.

"Right, right, sorry. You don't like to talk about that other power of yours. You know, at some point, you will have to let me in on the secret." Jewel took a bite of soup and looked up in thought. "I guess I'll just have to figure it out myself."

I smirked and shook my head. *I can't even figure it out. It might be Energy power, it might not. Who really knows?* I finally took a bite of my cooled-down food. A clacking of high heels near me made me cringe. *Belleza.*

"I hear they had to make a safety room for you so you could go and hide away," Belleza said in her high-pitched trill of a voice. "They were concerned that you're too dangerous, and can't control yourself. Isn't that right?"

Something in me clicked. As if someone had flicked on a light switch. I thought for a moment, then looked up at her with a curl on my lips. "Wanna find out?" I sassed.

Though she hid it well, I could see the confidence in her eyes fade into fear as I slowly stood up and faced her dead-on. "You wouldn't—

you don't even have the control," Belleza scoffed.

"Are you sure?" I said. It felt so good to see her face as she considered the possibility. She turned without another word and walked away.

I glanced at Jewel and flicked my eyebrows in amusement. She cracked a smile and giggled softly, gawking at the encounter. I sat back down, reveling in the feeling of accomplishment.

"Es, you don't actually have control over it yet, right? Or did I miss something?" Jewel noted.

"No. But, she doesn't know that," I said slyly. "I forgot how much fun it was to mess with her head." Someone walked close behind my chair. Their presence made my heart skip.

"Now, that's the Esmari that I know," Kasius said in a hushed tone as he leaned close to my ear. He flashed me a quick look of pride glinting in his black eyes, before continuing on his way out of the cafeteria.

I smiled sheepishly, feeling my heart pound in my chest. Slowly, I let out a breath. Jewel nudged me approvingly, letting out a giggle. I shook my head at her and finished my meal.

When I re-entered the classroom after lunch, Mr. Sean was by the near bookcase. He looked up for a moment, and I tossed him the packaged pastry I had brought from the cafeteria. He didn't say a word. He didn't have to. I knew he hadn't eaten anything other than the same old snack bars he seemed to have an endless supply of stashed away in his office.

The encounter with Belleza in the cafeteria gave me a feeling of confidence and intrigue about my Energy power. I found myself actually wanting to use my power, to explore it.

There were mixed feelings in my chest about it still, though. I couldn't quite tell if it was an anxious and excited feeling or a fearful feeling. The fact that Belleza was the one to bring it out of me added to the confusion. But, something in me was telling me that discovering this power would be the key. The key to what, I'm not sure, but I felt drawn to it.

"Well?" Mr. Sean's voice cut into my thoughts.

"What?" I shrugged.

"Mind Sight episode, or just zonin' out?" he asked, shoving the rest of the pastry in his mouth and crumpling the wrapper in his hand.

"Thinking," I said flatly. "You know what? I'm going to head to that uh, that room." I tossed a thumb over my shoulder, pointing to the door.

"Ah," he grunted. "Should I come with?"

"Uh," I hesitated. "No, no, I'm okay."

He nodded and turned away without any argument. In some way, that surprised me, but was also comforting, I think. I headed out of the classroom and down the hall.

Stepping into the Energy safe room, I took a look around. It was fairly empty, aside from a couple of chairs at the far side of the room. The walls were solid and plain, less for me to be able to accidentally destroy, I suppose. There were no windows to let outside light in, which made the room feel a bit eerie. The door of the classroom was made of solid, heavy wood, also plain. *Kind of feels like a box, doesn't it?* I smirked to myself, realizing the room had nicknamed itself. It was my box. *Sounds better than my "safe" room.* I shrugged to myself and shook my head.

Closing the door to the room, I flicked on all of the lights. They flickered on with a buzz. I realized they were one of the only things about the room that I might be able to break. *Definitely something to watch out for.* Taking a deep breath in, I walked to the center of the large room.

I suddenly had an epiphany. I had no idea where to begin. I hadn't found any materials to point me in the right direction. *How had I done it before? What made it activate?* I thought back. *Strong emotion? But that can't be the only way.*

Through my thoughts, I searched for the feeling it gave me. I focused on the sensation of it from within. *It had to have come from within me somehow.* An image of Hunter popped into my head, followed by Byrein. Immediately, I began to grow agitated. I could feel myself involuntarily dig my nails into the palms of my hands.

"No, get out of my head!" I growled at the memories.

Quickly, I looked down and saw the glow from my hands fade. *Maybe the strong emotions aren't the only way, but it's a good start.* I paused. I didn't want to face those emotions. I didn't want to relive those memories. It all felt like too much. Conflicted, I sat on the brick ground. I had gotten somewhere, much quicker than I expected, but not in a way I wanted to do again.

I stared at my blotchy pink palms. *Let's try this again.* I held onto the feeling that had just left my grasp. Trying hard, I traced the feeling back through my veins. For the first time, I thought about my power. How it breathed, how it moved. I focused on the sensation it gave each of my veins. The static feeling as it jolted through my bloodstream. I wanted it to happen. I wanted to experience it. I wanted to feel it in me, all the way to my fingertips.

Instinctively, I pressed my thumb firmly against my fingertips. In a silent snap, I flicked my thumb and fingertips away from each other, in the process causing the faintest flicker of light. My eyes grew wide and I smiled in amazement. *Did I really just do it?* I couldn't wait to try again. This time I pressed my fingers into my palm, then, in a sort of forcing manner, opened my fingers to reveal my palm, pushing this strong source of energy, of power, into my hand.

I could feel a flicker on my back just for a moment as my wings twitched with excitement. A glowing ball of power swirled in my hand, just as it had before. Adrenaline kicked in just as realization set in.

I forced more, trying to create a bigger orb of power. It grew brighter and brighter, soon engulfing my entire hand and part of my forearm.

Taking a deep breath, I let the power fade away, almost like a mist. I giggled with excitement. By instinct or accident, I had somehow figured it out. Definitely not in its entirety, but I had gotten somewhere.

I sat reveling in the moment of glee. I couldn't remember the last time I had truly felt this genuinely excited. I shook my head, still in awe of what had just happened. It was crazy and invigorating, and a rush. Part of me felt content, while part of me wanted to experience it again.

The exhilarating feeling became engulfed with fear as a flash of memory came back. My first experience with this power. I remembered the feeling of rage as I nearly killed a man. The conflict of emotions inside of me was exhausting and confusing.

But there was another feeling nagging at me, one I recognized stemming from the nape of my neck. My Mind Sight, so much easier to discern without my Energy power nagging, too. I welcomed it, placing my fingertips on the cool brick ground.

I didn't even take the time to close my eyes before my Mind Sight took over. My surroundings faded from view. It was a dark space at first. Then, I was watching someone. They were walking toward another person. They looked vaguely familiar.

One person turned, and I saw the shimmer of the letters ORP on their sleeve. They were speaking with each other in a hushed tone.

Slowly, their own surrounds came into view for me. They were standing near a desk, in an office of some sort. They continued to talk; I still couldn't hear what they were saying. One pointed to a paper on the desk. It faded into view. At the top was a picture of the Ex that attacked Hunter. The same one I nearly killed all those months ago. A red line was stricken through the rest of the paper. The one ORP, a lady, placed the paper in a bin labeled —

My surrounding came back into view, piece by piece. I felt groggy, lost. For a moment, I didn't remember where I was. *The box, right.* I took a slow, shaky breath. I didn't understand what I just saw. I tried hard to think back, to see where the paper was being filed. I didn't understand. My fingers played with the charm on my necklace, and a movement in the room caught my eye, making my heart skip.

Mr. Sean stood up from one of the chairs on the far side of the room. He rubbed at his neck and took a stretch before stuffing his hands in his pockets.

I looked up to the walls of my box room, finding no clock and feeling like my sense of time was missing. *How long had he been there?* The feeling of vulnerability set in.

"What did you see?" Mr. Sean inquired. I watched the shadow of his tattered wings on the wall behind him.

"Some people," I said nonchalantly. "And a paper being filed with a red strike through it."

Mr. Sean narrowed his eyes and looked me over. "With a picture on it?"

I nodded. "What does it mean when there's a red strike-through?" I asked, trying to keep a calm, unfazed tone. I didn't want him knowing how it all made me feel. Deep down, I was afraid of how he would hold it against me.

Mr. Sean sighed. "Usually that's how people like the ORP or Finders indicate that person has died," he explained. "Did you recognize the photo?"

I paused for a moment. "The Ex." I breathed. Looking at Mr. Sean's expression, I didn't need to explain further. There was a pause as I observed Mr. Sean's lack of movement.

Finally, he made a sharp nod of his head and started for the door. "That's plenty for today. Go home. Rest. No class tomorrow," he called over his shoulder, then left the room.

four

I walked in a sort of daze out of the academy. It was quieter than normal. When I swung open the front doors to exit, I realized just why that was.

It was late in the afternoon, and the sun was already beginning to set. *Just how long was I in the Sight episode?* I shook my head and folded my arms across my chest, trapping my cold hands against me. A breeze picked up as I walked carefully along the slushy walkway, trying not to fall. Making a mess of it, I decided to fly instead. At least I wouldn't be slipping and sliding all over.

I could see the glow of the streetlights kicking on all throughout Banshui, as I fluttered just high enough to pass over the trees. It felt good to stretch my wings, though I found the cold setting in more as the sun's last bit of warmth left the sky.

Before long, I arrived at the dorms and landed, unfortunately, in a puddle, which soaked straight through my shoes. *Definitely didn't make the correct choice in shoes for the day.* I frowned and sloshed my way into the building, being met with a warm wave of heat coming from the vents in the tiled lobby.

Stepping carefully, so I wouldn't slip on the already wet tile, I went toward the mail slot and found my room number. Thumbing through the letters, I took a deep breath. They were all from Athra. From Mom or Bray. I didn't have the energy to read them, though I rarely did on most days. I folded them over and tucked them away in my pocket.

I had such mixed feelings in my chest. The day had brought so many things to dwell on. Between the Ex and my Mind Sight, to my success with my Energy power, I didn't know how to feel.

On one hand, I was satisfied. The Ex had paid for what he had done to Hunter, with the ultimate price at that. I wasn't sure how he died, but what scared me a bit was that I was glad he did. *Does that make me as bad as an Ex?* I shook off the thought. Byrein's voice danced in my head once more like an unwelcomed performance, and I couldn't help wondering if Byrein had caused his death.

A sudden thought of my Energy power popped in my head. I remembered how it felt between my fingertips. How it felt coursing through my veins.

As I climbed the stairs, I tried to piece together this feeling I had of my Mind Sight and Energy being somehow connected. Mind Sight was the first power that had occurred and my Energy presented itself after. *But, how are they connected, Es? Did my Mind Sight bring out my Energy somehow?*

"Hey! Es!" Jewel called, skipping over to me. She had a warm grin on her face. "You're back late."

"Yeah, I was, uh, studying, sort of," I said, shifting in my sopping wet shoes.

She glanced at my feet pitifully and waved me to her room. "Did you get anywhere?" Jewel inquired cautiously.

I shrugged as I closed her door. "Yeah, I suppose I did."

"Really! That's great!" Jewel exclaimed.

I nodded out of habit at her words as I removed my shoes and peeled my wet socks from my feet. I went to her bathroom and hung them over the tub to dry. I crossed my arms, hearing the crinkle from the envelopes in my pocket as I leaned against the door frame. Jewel tossed me a towel and a clean pair of socks for my feet.

"Thanks," I mumbled, watching her step over to her round mirror hanging on the wall.

She began fussing with her hair in the reflection. "So, which was it?"

"Which what?" I asked.

"Power," she said. "Which power?"

I admired my friend for a moment as she swayed back and forth. The red-orange tips of her blonde hair were less vibrant than they once were. She pulled at the frayed ends of her soft curls, which were losing their bounce with the damp air, and frowned.

"Oh, uh, I think I got somewhere with my Energy power. I spent some time in the box."

"The box?" Jewel repeated quizzically.

"It's the nickname I have given my other classroom. It's like a big empty box." I laughed under my breath for a moment. *It sounds a bit silly, now that I am saying it out loud.*

"Cool, I like it. The box," Jewel approved with a reassuring nod. "Also, Energy power? Is that what your other power is? You haven't told me anything about it! I want to know! Wait, you said you got somewhere with it today, right? Does that mean you were able to, I don't know, uh, control it or something?"

I smiled softly at my friend, who was rambling. Her wings flittered ever so slightly whenever she did, which made her copper Royal's mark shimmer more noticeable on her left wing. Her blue eyes would get this twinkle in them as they glinted with excitement and passion over whatever she was going on about.

"I—" I stuttered. Thinking for a moment, I felt at a loss for words and explanations to satisfy her. My mind floated over the feeling using my Energy gave me. "Can I show you something?"

Jewel whirled around with excitement, clapping her hands. "Yes! Oh, please do!" she said eagerly.

"Okay, I don't know if it will work or not," I said, looking down. I felt an anxious excitement growing in me, yet it was still clouded with a fog of fear. I pointed across the room "Uh, stand over there, just in case."

She nodded and obeyed without hesitation. I could see a mixture of support and anxious terror in her eyes. Carefully, I slid up the sleeve of my sweater. Just as I had before, I focused on my Energy and forced it out into my hand. A quick spark of light later and I was holding a very small swirling ball of Energy, the size of a little river rock.

Jewel gasped at the sight. I didn't have the strength to hold it for long, and it quickly faded away like a mist. I smiled for a moment before a thought of Hunter popped in my head, and my contentment faded to a longing. *How I wish you were here to see this.*

Jewel came to me and placed her hands on my arms. "Thinking of Hunter again?" she asked softly.

I nodded as the sadness weighed down once again at my shoulders and crushed my chest.

"I know. He'd probably say something like,"

she lowered her voice and tried her best impersonation of Hunter, "'Whoa, that was wild!'"

I smirked at her sad attempt of Hunter's voice. But the words were spot on for something he would say. She flashed me a soft smile just as her phone rang. Quickly, she dropped her hands from my arms and danced merrily to answer it.

"Hello?—Oh, hi mom—sure—yep—yeah, tomorrow works—oh, and I'll bring a friend if that's okay?" Jewel eyed me.

I shook my head at her violently. "No," I whispered.

"Yeah?—Great!—She's very excited," she said, smiling at me slyly. I glared back and folded my arms across my chest. "Great! See you tomorrow!"

I took a sigh. "You're impossible."

I didn't want to risk it. Not with everything. Not without knowing really how to control things. And they may not like me. Trying to mind my manners and small talk with someone new? It sounded exhausting.

"Oh, come on, Es!" Jewel pleaded as she studied my face. "You'll like my parents. It would be good to get out of here for a bit. I certainly could use a change of scenery. Plus, they have heard so much about you, that it's about time they meet you. I mean, it's only fair. We can leave as soon as you are done with class."

I pressed my lips together and glanced at Jewel's begging eyes.

"I'm not taking no for an answer." Jewel stamped her foot down like a child throwing a tantrum.

I thought for a moment and sighed. I was free tomorrow, after all. She was right about one thing, it might be worth it to get out of the dorms, and away from here for a while.

"I don't have class tomorrow. I suppose I can go with," I muttered.

"Oh, even better! We can make a day out of it. You'll love my mom's salon. She does hair. Her timing is perfect because I need a trim. My hair is getting much too long, and all the split ends make it look like a beat-up paintbrush. You know, if you are ready for a change to your hair, my mom said she wouldn't mind fixing you up!" Jewel rambled. "And I'll show you around my old stomping grounds. We can have dinner at my parents' house, and you'll meet my dad. Just be aware, when he gets going on a topic he likes to talk about, he can go on forever! I just don't understand what gets into him, honestly. It's like he gets so excited that he has no control to pause for a breath!"

"Huh, sounds like someone else I know," I remarked sarcastically.

"What?" she asked. I could tell her own brain was catching up with what I had said. Suddenly, she furrowed her eyebrows at me. "Oh! Hey!"

I chuckled quietly, joining Jewel over by the mirror. She played with her hair and babbled about different options she had. After some time, she began to brainstorm what I could do with mine. Her genuine excitement over possible change was intriguing to me. She embraced the idea of change, welcomed it with open arms. I missed that about myself.

Lately, everything about my life has been "change." Change that was moving faster than I could keep up, let alone enjoy. But, not Jewel. It always seemed like everything was exciting to her. Even if it wasn't happening to her, but rather around her. She celebrated the "new," and was always excited to see what was next. The faster the change came, the more changes around her, the better.

Jewel and I spent the evening chatting about things from her childhood. More specifically, Jewel chatted and I listened to her stories and memories. At some point, I fell asleep in the big comfy bean bag chair and found myself replaying her stories in my dreams.

The following morning, Jewel and I set out towards West District. Jewel could hardly contain her excitement, though I wasn't sure if her excitement was over seeing her mom or dragging me along. Possibly both.

I, on the other hand, found myself nervous. *What would they think of me? Would they be afraid of me?* The thoughts running through my head were circling around, over and over, like the annoying merry-go-round that Hunter used to drag me on when the traveling fair came through Athra.

The snow was coming down lightly, flurrying around us as we flew. Jewel was jabbering on, once again, about different things that we might see in West District, or how it was different from Central District.

Every so often, she would look over to make sure I hadn't fallen behind, then continue on with her blabbering. Sometimes, I wonder if she even remembers to breathe when she talked so much. I like listening to her though; it gave me a sense of security in a way. And, she never minded if I responded or not.

We arrived shortly at an area littered with different businesses. It was a quaint area. Extraodinarily inviting and homey with all its small business. It reminded me of a more compacted version of my hometown, with businesses sitting side by side, sandwiched together, as well as a few floating overhead sporadically, casting their shadows on the walkways below. Jewel's mom's salon sat directly between a knickknack shop and what looked like a small jewelry store.

Entering inside the white French doors, we were met by a little chime coming from a dented metal bell hanging above the door. The pastel-colored walls and mismatched décor strewn about the salon gave off a much different feeling to the environment than I expected.

A taller woman with brown chunks in her straight short blonde hair came out of the backroom, rubbing the palms of her hands together. She had brushes and hairpins sticking off of the pockets of her black apron that swayed against her knees as she walked.

"Jewelei!" called the woman as she came to meet us at the door. She embraced Jewel in a warm hug before turning to me. "And you must be the friend she was bringing."

"Mom, this is Esmari. Esmari, this is my mom, Trina," Jewel introduced proudly.

"Hello," I said, nervously crumpling my sweatshirt sleeves into my fists down at my sides. I found myself tensing my arms and pressing my elbows into my ribs. Thankfully, Jewel and Trina didn't seem to notice.

"Welcome to my humble salon," she said, waving her hands as she admired the room. "I cleared my schedule just for you ladies today. So, let's get right to it. Jewelei, I'll start with you. And Esmari, you can come to take a seat right over here."

We followed Jewel's mom to one of the workstations. Jewel plopped down in the salon chair and nodded to me to take a seat in a golden painted chair along the wall. I slouched down in the seat, quietly observing as Trina got to work.

"You want the same or something different

today, sweetie?" Trina asked as she brushed through the knots in Jewel's hair.

"Same thing," Jewel answered.

"Sounds good," Trina nodded. "So Esmari, are you the friend who is in the dorm next to Jewelei?"

"Uh, yeah. That would be me," I said sheepishly.

"Mom, she's the one I told you about. The Mixer," Jewel noted. I looked at my hands, feeling embarrassed as I listened to the snaps being fastened on the black and white striped salon cape now draped over Jewel.

"Oh! A Mixer! That really is quite something." Trina began squeezing hair colors into different bowls and stirring them together with a color brush. Once she was satisfied with the mixture, she slowly began to spread it onto Jewel's hair. "So, what are you a mixer of?"

I felt odd answering these questions about me. "Mind Sight and Energy, I guess."

"Yeah, and she's getting better at it by the day, Mom! It's super cool. We even invented this game, maybe we can show you later! Dad would get a kick out of it too, I think." Jewel chattered happily.

"That would be nice," Trina smiled.

"Well, Jewel is getting pretty good at her ability too," I said, hoping to turn the conversation away from myself.

"That's good. I hope you are really focusing on practicing your ability, Jewelei. I know your father will be interested in seeing your progress. As am I, for that matter." Trina gathered up the bowls. "Okay, I'll be back. I need to wash these out."

Trina hustled away with the armful of color bowls. Jewel shifted in her seat, relaxing against the back. I found myself flicking at my fingers, creating a little Energy spark at the tips. I tried to see how small of a spark I could make and how long I could hold it, without it snuffing out. From the corner of my eye, I caught Jewel admiring.

"So, what are you going to do with your hair?" Jewel inquired.

I shrugged and looked at how silly she looked with her hair wrapped up in foils all around her head. She shifted again, causing the hairdresser's cape she had over her to make a swishing sound. I could see her deep in thought looking me over.

"What about something to match your wings?" she suggested.

I furrowed my eyebrows and looked at her

quizzically. "My wings are black. They look cracked and are uneven. So, what, I should have crazy, choppy, uneven black hair to match? I don't think that would look great," I stated coarsely, imagining it on myself.

"No, that wasn't what I was suggesting," Jewel sighed at my snarky comment.

"I mean, I do enjoy black, but I don't know about black hair." I pondered the idea.

"I meant one of the colors," Jewel said, shaking her head.

"The word you are looking for is 'black.' Unless you are referring to the copper smear, but I'm not too sure about having that color in my hair either." I chuckled.

"You don't know? Well, I guess it makes sense that you don't. I mean, they are on your back after all. How would you know? Unless you look in the mirror. And I'm sure you have never looked in the mirror while you did it..." Jewel's voice trailed off as she had a conversation with herself.

I kept staring at her as she continued on her debate. *Should I stop her? What is she even talking about?* Finally, she paused and looked at me.

"Do that thing you do. That thing you have

been doing with your fingers all day," she said vaguely.

"What? The Energy thing?" I asked.

"Yeah." Jewel nodded.

I looked at her, confused. Quickly, I flicked my fingers, sparking a small flare of energy at the tip of my pointer finger. "This?"

Jewel smiled widely and looked me over. She stood from her seat and came to me. After the flare had dispersed, she pulled gently at my arm, urging me to stand with a sly smile on her face. She pulled me over to stand in front of the salon chair and faced me to the mirror. Her mom came from the back and strode over to us.

Jewel glanced at her. "Mom, come over here. You have to see this," Jewel said. She nodded to me. "Go ahead. Do it again. But, look at your wings."

Jewel backed off slightly, giving me some room and joining her mother's side. I once again felt like I was some sort of display or show. It was a feeling I was growing used to, the more that people saw my abilities, but that didn't mean I liked it.

I took a breath and looked at Jewel again. She nodded once more to encourage me. I looked over my cracked black wings for a moment, not knowing what to expect.

Carefully, I flicked my thumb against my finger, creating a little spark, and held it on my fingertip. I glanced to my wings again and gasped in a small breath of awe. The broken-glass-like cracks were no longer hollow and black, but glowing with a similar light to the Energy spark that I held against my fingertips. I lost focus, and both my wings, and my hand, returned to normal.

I couldn't believe what I just saw. Quickly, I tried again. I flicked open my whole hand this time, holding a small sphere of Energy mist inside my palm, and looked again at my wings. It was incredible. The cracks were glowing like lightning which continued off the uneven ends of my wings, like a wafting mist, curving at the ends into a soft, rounded edge.

It was as if the part of my wings that was missing, was now there, glowing and beautiful. Like nothing I had ever seen before, but somehow reminding me of the wings of a monarch butterfly we would see every so often back in Athra.

My wings were rotating through different flickers of colors and a glow of Energy light. As I allowed the Energy in my palm to fade, so did the extension of my wings, returning them to their odd, broken-looking, black normalcy.

"How—when did you know?" I stuttered, looking at Jewel with confusion-riddled eyes.

She smiled at me. "That day you accidentally knocked me to the ground with that surge. I thought I saw them glow that day. But, when we were talking to Mr. Sean, and then when you showed me that thing yesterday, they were glowing then too," Jewel explained. "I just thought you knew."

I shook my head, still in disbelief. "No." I thought for a moment. "Does this happen when I am in a Sight episode?"

"No, not that I've seen. Just with your Energy power, I think," Jewel noted, shaking her head. The foils in her hair swished against each other.

"Okay, it's been enough time, I think your hair is ready to wash out," Trina said, pulling open some of the foils in her hair to check. She nodded her head to herself in satisfaction before leading Jewel over to the sinks.

I returned to my chair, still mulling over what I had just seen. Had Jewel not told me, I would have had no idea that my wings were not just the awkward-looking black things on my back.

I actually liked them. In a matter of moments, I completely changed my outlook on them. *But if it only happens when I use my Energy power, what does that mean exactly?* I frowned to myself for a split second. I wasn't going to let that damper my newfound intrigue about my own wings. I took a breath and pictured my wings in all their glowing beauty.

Jewel and Trina returned happily chatting away. Trina sat Jewel down and began trimming at Jewel's hair. I listened contently to their chatter. Jewel rambled on about different things that were happening in her class, telling her mom about lessons she was looking forward to, and silly stories of mishaps.

She even included a story about being praised by her teacher while Belleza and Lilly did not, which made me chuckle just thinking of their jealous scowls. A dull ache in the back of my neck began and quickly moved up to the nape of my neck. I sighed and tried to massage it away.

Jewel glanced at me with kind, understanding eyes. "Do you want to show my mom that game we do?"

I thought for a moment and chewed at my lip. "No, maybe later. I think I'll just step out for a second," I said, flashing a quick smile at her.

"Sounds good!" she agreed.

"Careful, it's pretty cold out there," Trina cautioned, nodding to the door.

I nodded back and attempted a comforting smile, before stepping out the door. Trina was right, it was chilly. Tiny snowflakes stuck to my sleeves as I crouched to the ground. I rubbed my hands together and tried to warm them for a moment longer, knowing very well just how cold they would be after the episode was done.

I took a slow, steady breath and placed my fingertips gently against a small spot of crisp concrete clear of snow. I closed my eyes and listened as my surroundings fell away.

I saw a figure walking. A man, who looked familiar. I didn't feel uneasy, I felt comfortable looking at him. He turned and smiled. *Finn*. He seemed nearby.

A shiver shook through me, and I blinked back into reality. Cuffing my hands together, I brought my nearly frozen fingertips to my mouth and blew warm air onto them.

I stood up and looked around. Finn's eyes met mine from across the way, with Moz and Darren just behind him. They came to a halt and, for a moment, just stood, unsure of how to proceed.

I sighed and smiled at Hunter's old roommates. Softly, I brought up a hand and waved to them. Finn smiled back, and they made their way over to greet me. Surprisingly, I found my heart warmed to see their familiar faces.

"Hey, Es," Finn greeted gently.

I nodded back. "Hi, guys."

"Uh, how are you?" Finn asked cautiously.

"I'm doing okay. It's really good to see you guys," I said. For some reason, I expected it to hurt more seeing them. That I would be angry or feel guilty. That it would rip me apart. But instead, I found myself feeling quite the opposite. I felt comfortable. Happy, even.

"It's great to see you too, Es," Moz chimed. Darren nodded affirmatively.

"How's it going for you? How are your internships and stuff?" I asked, feeling as though I were stumbling over my words.

"Pretty good. I actually just got back into mine.

They gave me some time off in light of everything. I had to wait until I got my arm cast off too, which took a bit longer than expected," Finn explained. A quick memory of Finn holding his limp arm the day the Ex attacked their house popped in my head. I sighed as I watched Finn wave his hand around, showing off how well he had healed. "But, it's all back to working condition now, and I'm getting back into everything. Moz and Darren are still figuring their lives out, though."

"Hey!" Moz scoffed. "I'll have you know that I was recently observing under a guy who works with the Historical Documentation Department."

"You fell asleep in the office," Darren teased.

Moz pursed his lips and nodded slowly to agree. "Okay, yeah, I did. Still into History, maybe just not filing and working with all those dusty old papers." He shrugged. Suddenly, he turned to Darren with a mocking expression. "What have you done, Darren?"

Darren pressed his lips together. Embarrassed, he looked at me and changed the subject. "How're your studies going?"

"Uh, good, sort of," I said with a furrowed brow.

"Es!" Jewel called from behind me as she emerged from the salon. Her face lit up at the sight of our small gathering. "Oh! Hey! It's been a while, guys!"

"Hi, Jewel!" Finn said, his voice laced with excitement. He rubbed the back of his neck nervously. "You, uh, you look good!"

"Thanks! My mom just fixed my hair up for me!" She shivered. "Brr! It's cold out here! Hey, I hate to break this reunion up, but Mom's ready for you, Es."

Moz shrugged. "It's cool, we have to get going anyway."

"See you two around?" Finn asked hopefully.

"Yeah, keep in touch! Our numbers are still the same," Jewel mentioned with a quick wave of her hand.

We turned back to the salon and Jewel reached to the door handle.

"Hey, Es?" Finn called. I looked back at his face. He was fighting the words inside.

"Yeah?" I prompted.

"I—It's just—I—" Finn stuttered. He shook his head. "I miss him too."

"I know," I breathed.

We waved them goodbye, and Jewel pulled me back inside the warm shop. We stamped off the snow from our shoes, and I brushed the melting snowflakes from my sleeves. Jewel shook her shiny fresh-looking hair with her hands to dust off the water droplets and smiled to me as we rejoined Trina.

"Okay, Esmari. What should we do with your hair?" Trina thought aloud as she brushed through my tangled mess.

I looked myself over in the mirror before me as I relaxed back into the cushion of the salon chair. I felt refreshed seeing Hunter's old roommates. Trina stepped back for a moment and stuck her hands on her hips with thoughts riddled on her face.

I looked at my hands and flicked a puff of Energy from my finger the size of a pea. I watched as the bright flicker of color wafted away into the air, just inches in front of me.

"I don't know," I mumbled as I flicked off another puff of energy. "I think I am ready for something new."

"New, you say?" Trina said, still deep in thought.

I looked at Jewel momentarily. She smiled

softly back. "Something bold?" I offered.

Jewel nodded her head affirmatively at me. "But still you," she noted. Her face lit up with an idea, and she scurried over to her mom. Quickly, she whispered into Trina's ear, and I watched as Trina's face also lit up with excitement.

"Yes! Perfect," Trina agreed. "Okay, Es, be ready to be transformed into the new you!"

I looked at Jewel and smiled nervously. My heart leaped with anxious excitement as Trina turned my chair around, facing me away from the mirrors, saying how she wanted it to be a surprise.

She got right to work mixing bowls of color and slathering them onto different parts of my hair. It was the first time I had someone work on my hair like this, and I found it momentarily relaxing.

While we sat, Jewel and her mom chatted away about different things. I sat contently listening. Every so often, they would ask my opinion about this and that, and then continue to chat on.

I learned all about how West District used to be. How much had changed over the years. Trina would mention different ideas of places to show me to Jewel, which would start them on another tangent of stories of the past.

Before I knew it, Trina was finishing with my hair. I found myself growing more and more anxious to see what I was going to look like. She dried my new locks and combed them through. It felt soft and light. Definitely, shorter than when I came in, but for some reason, that didn't make me nervous. It felt refreshing. Lighter, almost.

"Okay, time for the reveal!" Trina sang.

She spun me around to face the mirror and stepped back to admire her masterpiece. I looked over myself in the mirror.

It felt like I was looking at a whole different person. I ran my fingers through my soft strands of collarbone-length hair and watched as the subtle pastel-colored highlights peeked out for a moment, only to become hidden when my natural blonde hair settled over top. The fringy layers lay perfectly all over, giving me an overall edgy look.

"Do you like it?" Trina asked.

I smiled and nodded. "Yes. It's perfect."

"The colors were inspired by your wings," Jewel mentioned.

I flicked a puff of Energy and observed the similarities of colors in my new hair. I didn't quite understand why, but I felt somehow reassured. Like I was beginning to see a newfound confidence in myself. Something I didn't even realize I was missing from my life up until that point. It was unfamiliar, but I found myself enjoying the feeling.

Somehow, in the middle of this little salon, I started to see the true me.

Jewel and I enjoyed our new looks in the mirror together for a few more minutes as we tried different hairstyles we could achieve. After the snow let up a bit outside, we thanked Trina and went out exploring the West District.

Jewel took me on a tour of several different areas where she grew up, noting several times how different things had changed in such a short time. Every so often, I would catch a glimpse of my reflection in a store window and smile to myself.

five

We arrived at Jewel's parents' home that evening as the snow began to come down heavily. It was magical to see as it glittered in the golden porch lights of their quaint, cottage-looking home.

Two large trees sat framing the sides of the house, their branches covered in a layer of fresh powdered snow. Icicles hung off the wooden railing of the steps up to their front door.

We entered the heavy wooden front door and

stamped our shoes off on the brown woven mat in the entryway. The two of us slid out of our wet-soled shoes and placed them on a plastic tray to the side to dry out.

A waft of the roast Trina was slicing graced our nostrils as we entered the bright kitchen. Jewel's eyes twinkled at the familiarity of home.

I, on the other hand, felt awkward and out of place. I tugged at my sleeves uncomfortably. A pressure in the back of my neck urged at me, and I shifted my weight, swaying from side to side as if it would ease the sensation. It didn't.

"Go wash up, girls. Dinner is just about ready. Jewelei, your father will be home soon, and we will eat," Trina instructed.

I found myself staring at the floor with a clenched jaw as my Sight pressured me. Jewel tugged at my elbow with a cool fingered hand. I followed her down a small dark hallway, plastered with family photos in mismatched frames, to a candle lit bathroom that smelled of cinnamon.

"You okay?" Jewel asked as she dried her hands on a tattered-looking towel. I pressed my lips into a forced smile and nodded.

Quickly, I tucked my tangled hair behind my

ear and scrubbed my hands clean. Shaking the excess water from my hands, I looked up at my reflection in the round mirror and took a deep breath. *Later. Just let me have a good meal, and I'll use you later, okay Mind Sight?* As if my Mind Sight had listened and obeyed, the nagging sensation at the nape of my neck lessened. My eyes widened out of surprise and relief as I smirked to myself quietly.

"What?" Jewel asked, glancing over my face.

I shook my head. "Nothing," I said with the smile still lingering on my lips. We rejoined Trina as the front door opened, letting in a gust of brisk winter air.

"Hi, dear. I'm home!" called a deep, exhausted-sounding voice.

Jewel flashed me a look and linked my arm with hers. She pulled us eagerly out of the kitchen and to the entryway, where we found a very surprised-looking man. He grinned widely at the sight of his daughter. Tossing down the briefcase in his hand, he unbuttoned his wet-shouldered beige coat and shrugged it off.

"Well, now, if it isn't my little girl?" he said, pinching softly at her cheek.

Jewel winced and pulled away. "Dad!" she

wined. "I'm not a little girl anymore."

"Okay, okay," he sighed. His thinning hair lay messy on the top of his head, glistening with droplets of now-melted snowflakes. "You must be the friend she has been telling us all about."

"Hello, I'm Esmari," I greeted. My voice sounded off. Rehearsed, and anything but genuine. Thankfully, no one seemed to notice but me.

"Nice to meet you, I'm Ludrex. Feel free to call me Rex. Most people do," he noted, shaking my hand firmly. "Now, what is it that your mom has made that smells so good, Jewelei?"

"Her roast," Jewel said, raising her eyebrows. A twinkle glinted in her eye as she peered at her father before her.

"Oh! What a treat!" Rex chuckled with excitement.

We all entered a small dining room, just large enough for the wooden table and chairs, and almost no walking room to spare. Trina untied her apron and hung it on the back of her chair as she sat down. Rex pecked his wife on the cheek before taking a seat next to her. He unbuttoned the sleeves of his dress shirt and rolled them up to his elbows.

Jewel and I sat opposite of them. I awkwardly

tried to scoot in my chair, but after two failed attempts, I left it alone and perched on the edge of the seat instead. My wings dusted the edges of the cool wooden chair below me. Jewel dished up some food for the both of us and handed me a napkin before digging in.

"How was work?" Trina asked Rex.

"Still getting the situation under control. I think it will likely take another several days. Let alone all the paperwork involved," Rex said, shaking his head and taking a large bite of the roast.

Jewel leaned over and whispered in my ear. "Dad works for a small division in a water company. They had an issue with some piping lately at a local project because of the cold temperatures."

"How about you, many clients today?" Rex mumbled through a bite of food.

"Don't talk with your mouth full, Rex, we have a guest, remember?" Trina scolded, shaking her head. "I had a few appointments today, but I did get to do the girls' hair today! Don't they look lovely?"

"You girls are always changing your hair," Rex

chuckled.

"Dad, you're just jealous because all of your hair is falling out!" Jewel teased.

Rex flashed her a glare, pointing at her with a potato-ended fork, then a moment later rolled his eyes and nodded in agreement. He sighed and snatched the potato chunk from the prongs of his fork with his teeth.

Trina and Jewel flashed a look to each other and giggled. The encounter reminded me of home. I cut at a piece of roast and swallowed back the memories.

"So, Esmari, Jewelei tells us that you two are neighbors at the dorm?" Rex chimed.

"Uh—yeah. I was assigned the dorm next to hers when I arrived. It's been really nice." I smiled anxiously as I played with the hem of my sleeve inside my balled-up fist under the table. My other hand held a metal fork hovering over a piece of roast.

"And what are you studying?" he asked. "What's your power?"

"Oh, um. I'm—um—I'm a Mixer," I stuttered, shoving a chunk of soft potato in my mouth and looking down at my plate full of warm food.

"Yeah, Dad! It's so cool. She's a Sight, a Mind Sight and has Energy or something too," Jewel bragged cheerily.

"Well, now that is interesting," Rex said.

"Yeah, definitely more exciting than my power, that's for sure. Tell, them, Es!" Jewel pressed.

I felt that all-too-familiar feeling of being on display for everyone. "It's kind of hard to explain, honestly. They, I mean the people at the school, originally thought I was a Distance Sight."

"What's the difference?" Rex prompted.

"Well, I guess a Distance Sight can see far away stuff. Like having really good vision, or having a pair of binoculars that you can activate in a sense. But, after some time, we discovered that I was really a Mind Sight, instead," I attempted to explain, but even I felt like my explanation was a bit on the vague side.

"Huh," Rex said, trying to understand. I could see him mulling over the information.

"Basically, instead of seeing it with my eyes, I see things inside my head. Sort of. And it doesn't have to be near me. It can be outside of the building that I'm in, or I can see across the town, into another building, even." I searched for the right words to explain to the curious eyes watching me. "Yeah, it's difficult to explain. I'm the one with the Mind Sight, and even I have a hard time understanding it sometimes."

Rex paused for a moment, then gave out a hearty chuckle. Which surprisingly made me feel more at ease. "That sounds like quite the power to have!"

"It's interesting to see. Oh! We should show them the trick we do!" Jewel boasted.

"Trick?" Rex asked, raising an eyebrow with curiosity.

"Yeah. We came up with a game that we do. It helps when Es needs to use her power. It also helped her learn how to control her power more. Well, her Mind Sight anyway. But it's really fun for the both of us," Jewel rattled off. I smiled to myself, knowing I was out of the woods from needing to talk for a little bit. "So, I went with her to her class a while back and she was still learning how to control her power, and so, just for fun, we came up with this game to see if it would help. And, well, anyway, we will have to show you. It ended up working pretty well. Now, we do it all the time."

"That sounds interesting. You've got me intrigued, that's for sure," Rex said with a kind smirk.

"Yeah, I get to exercise my power at the same time, which is cool too," Jewel continued, only to pause long enough to shove the last bit of her food in her mouth. She swallowed hard, barely chewing. "So, I take some kind of liquid, usually water, it's less messy if things get out of hand, and I take and form that water into any shape or thing I can think of. Actually, I'm getting pretty good at creating things. Better than I used to be, I think. Wouldn't you say so, Es?"

I looked to my friend and nodded. "Yeah."

"So, where does Esmari come in? How is it a game for the two of you?" Trina asked.

"Oh, right, right, sorry, sidetracked," Jewel sighed, shaking her head. I chuckled quietly. "Well, she tells me what I made. With the water, that is. And, you know, using her Mind Sight and stuff. Why don't we just show them?"

"Sure." I smiled. I figured she would get around to asking me sooner or later. The nagging at the back of my neck had returned, leaving a dull ache in my shoulders. *Perfect timing, too, Jewel.*

"Okay, cool, I'll be here, and I'll just turn around," Jewel said.

I looked around once again at the small space surrounding the table. *Not much room to crouch by the ground, is there, Es?* I stood and walked to the doorway instead and knelt on the floor, facing away from her. "Ready when you are."

"Okay, what is it?" she called over.

I took a breath. Closing my eyes, I gently placed my fingertips against the ground. The water in her hands became clear inside my head. "A flower," I stated. She moved, and I watched again as she formed the water.

"How about now?" she asked.

"A house," I answered.

"Fascinating!" Rex gawked. "Truly, truly fascinating!"

I opened my eyes and touched my necklace for a moment as I stood to my feet. The nagging at my nape lessened, but was still present. *Later, I promise.* Suddenly, the ache faded to the point that I barely noticed it any longer. Pleased, I returned to my seat.

"Pretty cool, huh?" Jewel said, barely sitting still in her seat from the excitement.

"Yes, that's quite the trick you two ladies can do," Trina noted as she began collecting our empty plates. She disappeared out of the room and we could hear the clatter of the plates in the kitchen sink as she began to wash them.

"I'm getting better, aren't I, Dad?" Jewel said, searching his face for approval.

"That house actually looked like a house this time, Jewel," I teased, nudging her.

"Okay, okay." She rolled her eyes at me.

"No, no. She's right. It really did look like a house. You know, when Jewel was just starting out with her ability, she used to try to make all sorts of shapes. She'd insist that they were this thing or that, but they either looked like blobs or fell out of her hands altogether. She was never really the most artistic of children." Rex smiled. With a raise of an eyebrow, he lifted his cup to his lips and took a smug sip.

"Dad!" Jewel frowned.

I smirked at the encounter. Rex reminded me a bit of Dad. *They would get along well.*

An unexpected, quick twinge in the nape of my neck struck. I drew a sharp breath in out of surprise and clasped a hand against it. I squeezed my eyes shut and fiddled with the black stone of my necklace. A cool touch fell against my shoulder.

"It didn't satisfy it. Go ahead, out to the living room." Jewel nodded to the doorway.

I looked at her with sorrowful eyes. "I'm sorry, I don't want to be rude," I whispered.

"No, it's okay. Really. I'll check on you in a little bit," Jewel urged.

I sighed and nodded, excusing myself from the room. I could hear Jewel quietly explaining to her father what was going on. I was grateful for her eagerness to explain for me.

I found my way into the quaint living room. A dim lamp in the corner of the room reflected on a small clock sitting on the fireplace mantle. *Just before seven.* I noted the time down in my head as I sat on the decorative rug in the center of the room.

I felt my wings brush against the textured fabric couch behind me. Slowly, I took a breath and calmed my mind before closing my eyes. Gently, I placed my fingertips against the area beneath me and felt the frayed fibers from the worn rug against the edges of my fingernails. I welcomed the feeling of a surge of power leaving my fingertips, sending me into my Sight episode.

I could see figures, two of them, facing each other. They were mostly silhouetted, aside from the occasional flicker of light caused by a nearby fire. They were speaking to each other, whispering almost too low to hear.

The firelight flickered again, I could see a man's face, one I didn't recognize. He was holding out a sketch. Slowly, the graphite on the paper became clearer. It was of storefronts. It looked familiar, covered in snow. *The salon.*

I caught a word from a familiar voice. "Wait." I strained to hear more of what he was saying. The more I strained, the more I felt like I was being pulled away.

My surroundings came back to me. The beads of sweat forming on my neck were like ice in the cool air. The voice was Byrein's, I was sure of it. *Wait? Wait for what?* I didn't like the feeling I was getting down in my gut.

They had a sketch of the very salon that Jewel and I were at just earlier that day, the one Jewel's mom works at every day. *Were they following us?*

My head was spinning with anger and confusion. My arms and shoulders were stiff from sitting so tensely for as long as I had.

A ticking from the clock reminded me to account for my time. I stretched my neck for a moment and looked once again at the little golden hands to the clock residing on the mantle. *Eight-twenty.* I had lost over an hour this time.

I didn't like the feeling that the episode gave me. Were they watching me? Were they following me? I felt as though Jewel was in danger, her family, too. *Do they know her mom's a Non-Royal?*

An all too vivid memory of Hunter's limp hand in mine made me feel sick. I didn't want to experience that again, let alone, allow my friend to. All I knew was that I didn't want to be there. I wanted to run away, fly away, as fast as I possibly could. I stood and gathered myself, shaking the numb feeling from my left foot.

My head flooded with thoughts, all so chaotic I couldn't catch my breath. I needed out. I needed to escape. *Why did I have to see that? Why was I drawn to see that? How long had they been inside of Banshui? What were they waiting for? For me to notice them? For more of them to notice me?* One thing I knew for certain was that I was being watched. If I could just get away, disappear, maybe I could protect Jewel and her family.

"Es?" Jewel's voice from the doorway made me jump. "You okay?"

I nodded and bit my lip, trying to hide the chaos swirling still in my head.

"You were there a while." Jewel's voice was soft and kind towards me, as usual. I don't know why, but it stung to hear her kindness.

Byrein's voice crept into my ears once again. I clenched my teeth. "Hey," I started.

"Oh, yeah, Dad got word that the school is closed for the next of couple days. Frozen pipes and something to do with the snow on the roof," Jewel noted. She took a sip from her steaming mug. "Do you want a cup? It's mom's hot cocoa. Warms you up right down to your toes. I figured since there's no class—"

"Jewel, I, uh," I started.

"—we could just go back in the morning. It's really coming down out there, you know," Jewel continued.

"Jewel, actually, I think I may go," I finally said, taking a shaky breath.

"What? Why?" Jewel stammered.

"I just—"

"It has something to do with your Sight

episode, doesn't it?" Jewel pressed.

"I—" It felt like my tongue and my teeth were not cooperating to form a sentence. *Why is it so hard to talk to her?*

Jewel shook her head. "The storm's picking up out there. We can just stay here and relax some. Consider it a little vacation."

"Jewel."

"What happened in your episode this time? Do you want to talk about it?" she asked.

"Jewel, I don't want to talk about it. I just think I should go," I mumbled.

"Why? You were having a nice time, right? I was right, it has something to do with the Sight episode. I'll get you some cocoa and you can tell me all about it," Jewel rambled on.

"Jewel, I don't want to," I tried. I could feel myself becoming more and more irritated. *Why was she pressing me?*

"No, you don't need to leave. It's too cold out tonight," Jewel protested.

"Jewel, it wasn't a question. I don't need your permission," I breathed hotly.

Jewel looked at me with pleading eyes. "You don't need to run away. I just want to help."

"You can't help!" I snapped. "Jewel, you don't understand."

"Help me understand!" she snapped back, taking a step toward me. I could see the rage boiling in her eyes.

"I'm not doing this right now. You can't understand," I breathed hotly through my teeth.

I pushed just past her, and she snagged my elbow with her dainty hand. Without thinking, I yanked away, nearly causing her to spill her mug of cocoa on herself. She drew a sharp breath of frustration.

"Why do you do this? Why do you keep running away? I'm trying to be patient. I really am. I'm trying to be here for you. I'm trying to understand and let you heal. But you just keep pushing me and everyone else away. I know I'm not Hunter. I feel like no one will be good enough!" Jewel blurted, her face growing more and more red as each word left her mouth. "You act like you are all alone. Like you are the only one who has ever lost anyone. Hunter is gone, Es. You can't change that. I know. But, at some point, you have to move on. Hunter is the one who died, not you. And you are sitting around wasting your life. Wasting your potential. Wasting your rare abilities. Hunter died at the hand of an Ex for you, and you make it up to him by wasting your life and abilities! So many Royals would give anything to be as powerful as you are. But here you are, just wasting it. Quite frankly, I think Hunter would have been just as disappointed as I am in you!"

Jewel gasped at her own words and threw a hand over her mouth. "Oh, Es—"

"How dare you," I sneered, my face hot with a mix of anger and embarrassment. I dug my nails into my hands and suppressed my Energy power from escaping my veins.

"Es," Jewel gasped.

I turned and stormed to the door. I didn't want to hear it. *How could she! I know more than anyone that Hunter was gone. I needed him here. I needed someone to be here and understand. I needed his goofy smile and his excitement. I did not need the reminder that my best friend was dead. I don't need her reminding me about being a disappointment. That I don't belong. That I am a waste.* I shoved my shoes on and heard Jewel's mug clank as it hit the glass top of the nearby side table.

"Es, I'm sorry. I—I'm sorry— I didn't—" Jewel

stammered, chasing after me.

"Didn't what? Didn't mean it? Or didn't mean to actually say it out loud? Because you obviously were thinking it," I scoffed. My face hot with anger, I swung open the door and a cold breeze kissed my cheeks.

"Es, come on. It's freezing and the storm is getting worse. Come back in. Please? We can talk it through!" Jewel begged from the doorway, still in her socks.

I stepped away from the porch, my back still to her. Slowly, I sighed. "I need some time to think," I said finally.

Glancing over my shoulder for a moment, the world slowed down. A gust of wind blew a few snowflakes in her direction and she hugged her shivering arms to her chest. Her fresh-cut hair lay just at her shoulders, swaying back and forth from the brisk breeze.

Jewel curled her toes inside her mismatched socks as she peered back at me with pleading blue eyes. I could see the tears welling up in her eyes as they glinted in the light seeping from inside the warmth of her home.

I was confused inside. Like my emotions were

battling. Anger, sadness, fear. I didn't know what to feel.

Another trembling breath escaped my lips. Byrein's unwelcomed voice echoed in my head once more. "Wait." I scrunched my eyes shut and shook my head slightly, as if his words would rattle from my brain. *I can't lose you, too, Jewel. Even if you are disappointed in me. Maybe it's for the best that you are.*

Without another word, I stretched my tense wings out and left the snow piled ground just outside Jewel's home behind me.

It was hard to see through the massive amounts of snow dumping out of the sky. I didn't care. I just felt lost and confused. I didn't know where I was heading. I just was flying. Barely feeling the snowflakes as they melted against the warmth of my wings.

My conversation with Jewel replayed over and over in my head as I flew through the chilly night sky. I cringed to myself at the way I snapped at her.

There was such a mixture of emotions brewing inside my chest, I didn't know just what I was supposed to feel. I wanted to take back my words to her. I wanted to go back in time and make sure our conversation never happened. At the same time, I was angry and upset with her. I had so much bitterness toward her words.

It was extraordinarily quiet in the world below me as I flew. I almost wished there was noise, so there would be some sort of distraction from my own thoughts. My cheeks began to grow numb from the freezing air constantly being pressed against them. The lights from the neighborhoods below twinkled against the fresh snowflakes flurrying in the air.

A shiver shook through me, all the way to the tips of my wings. It became more and more difficult to fly. I wasn't sure if it was because I was tired, or because of the temperature growing increasingly colder against my wings. *Maybe I should have just stayed.*

A flicker of the salon's storefront crossed my mind accompanied by Byrein's voice once more. I squeezed my eyes shut and shook my head. *No. Go away.* I wanted more than anything to just disappear. I wanted to run away from myself and what I was becoming. *Maybe leaving is for the best.*

My wings faltered, feeling half-numb with cold, and making me dip in altitude. I gasped and looked down at the ground so far below me. I didn't know where I was. I didn't even know what direction I was flying any longer. Fear washed over me, feeling completely alone. Another shiver rippled through me.

"You've got to find someplace to warm up for a bit, Es," I whispered warily to myself.

Looking around at the surroundings, I drifted closer and closer to the ground. My wings ached from the frigid air as I placed my feet against the freshly powdered mound of snow on top of what used to be a pathway.

I couldn't see any signs through the thick snowflakes falling into the darkness. Slowly, I took a shaky breath and shoved my hands under my arms, hugging myself for warmth. I wandered towards the direction of possible lights I had seen while up in the night sky. Each step seemed more daunting than the rest as my legs and toes grew colder. *Athra never was this cold in the winter.*

My mind wandered to my hometown. I

thought of the bare trees hanging over the paths as a dry, crisp breeze would make the red clay dirt dance around at our feet.

Bray and Mom were probably making cookies. More likely, Mom was making the cookies, and Bray would be helping by licking the spoon. Dad would probably be sitting over by the fireplace, adding in another piece of wood. Hunter would be…

I sighed to myself as I continued to shuffle along, allowing the memories to turn to tears in my eyes. My heart ached for the simple times back in Athra as I suppressed a shiver. I wiped the chilly tears from my cheeks with my shoulder, afraid that if I didn't, they'd turn to ice on my skin. I could have been fine without ever experiencing a single winter in Banshui.

A chime from what sounded like a bell on a shop door echoed into the night, giving me the slightest glimmer of hope, and I wandered my way toward the origin. A shadow of a person flew over me, but I didn't have the strength to look up, growing more desperate to feel warmth, and, quite frankly, my toes too.

"Well, my fluttering flitters!" said a boisterous

voice as it landed just a few feet in front of me.

I looked up and squinted through the downpouring snow, shivering once more. My body ached from the cold.

"Are you alright?" asked the voice. An older woman in a fluffy, red coat came into view. "You look like you are about to be frozen into a statue! Let's get you out of this cold."

I didn't object. I didn't have the energy to even open my jaw and say anything. For that matter, I don't even think I could so much as manage a nod to accept. The strange woman took me by the shoulders and guided me into a nearby café with the words "Redd's Place" on the glass of the door.

It was brightly lit inside from the floressent lights overhead, with mismatching wooden tables and chairs strewn about. Off to one side, a person was adjusting a microphone stand next to an empty metal stool.

There were only a couple of other people inside, likely because of the storm brewing outside. One person glanced at me, but only for a moment, before ducking his head back down and taking another bite of his steaming bowl of soup. I found that I didn't care much about any of this because, most importantly, it was warm inside the little café.

"Come on, let's get you something warm to drink," the woman said, leading my still-ridged body to one of the stools at the bar. A man came out of a swinging half-door that led to a kitchen area, based on the aroma he wafted towards us.

"Jan!" called the man happily. The lights above shone off of his shiny bald head. "I didn't think we would see you tonight with this storm out!"

"Well, Redd, I wasn't planning on it. I found this one half-frozen just outside," the woman noted, jutting a manicured thumb in my direction. She shrugged off her coat and draped it across the stool beside her, revealing her decorative, sapphire blue blouse. She seemed dressed too elegantly for a place like this, but who was I to argue?

"Well, let's get you something to warm you up, miss?" Redd said. I nodded, though I think it was a rhetorical question. "And, are we having the same as usual, Jan?"

"Nope, going to have one of Bill's drinks tonight," Jan said with a twinkle in her hazel-colored eyes. She smoothed a stray strand of short gray hair and tucked it behind her ear, uncovering some fancy, purple-stoned earrings.

"Oh! Is it already the anniversary? How long has it been now?" Redd's voice beckoned from the drink station as he prepared my mystery drink. His plain ruby-colored wings flicked on his back as steam puffed into his face, revealing a copper smear on the bottom left wing. *Royal.* Not that it mattered, but also, not what I had expected.

"Six years gone now," Jan stated proudly. I adjusted myself in my seat and observed the conversation as I felt the tingle of warmth returning to my feet and the tips of my wings.

Redd set a mug of hot water, as well as a plate with a lemon and a couple of teabag choices in front of me to choose from. I picked a simple green tea and began to seep it in the water, warming my hands over the steam as it rose from my mug.

"Thank you," I managed to say.

"You just get yourself warmed up," he nodded, handing Jan a mug with two cinnamon sticks sticking out of it.

Redd lifted a mug of the same drink that Jan had, cinnamon sticks and all. "To Bill," he said. The two of them touched their mugs together with a clank and took a slurp of the steaming liquid inside. Redd set his mug aside and nodded toward us with a smile on his rosy cheeks, before returning to the kitchen.

I finally removed the tea bag from my well-steeped tea and set it aside on the plate. I took a slow sip of the hot liquid and enjoyed the instant warmth it brought to my chest.

Cautiously, I glanced again at Jan sitting beside me as she swirled the drink in the cup, watching the cinnamon sticks slide around the opening of the mug like a silly dance. She smiled to herself.

"Miss you, Hun," she whispered, almost inaudibly.

Her eye caught mine, and I looked away, feeling guilty, as if I was looking in on her private moment with a special person.

I heard her sigh happily. "It was my Bill's favorite drink. Half coffee, half hot chocolate, a touch of vanilla, and two cinnamon sticks."

"Was he special to you?" I asked, hesitantly.

She nodded. "He was my husband. Married almost fifty years, we were. He passed away six years ago. He was something, my Bill. I celebrate with his drink every year on the anniversary of his death." She took another gulp of the drink.

"You celebrate?" I asked. *Was she happy he's gone?*

"Well, celebrate his life, his time with me. People die. We can't dwell on their death and forget to live our life! If we do, we are just wasting away our time, our life! If we do that, what's the point of even being alive, we are as good as dead too!" Jan said, letting out a boisterous laugh. She shook her head at the thought.

I thought for a moment. It was as if she were unintentionally lecturing me on Hunter's death. Her words reminded me of Jewel's. She made it sound so easy. To just move on. To look at it as a celebration of their life, rather than grieve their absence from your own life.

I didn't know how to take it. Though, it seemed different. I found myself envying the long life this Bill was allowed, and all of the years Hunter was robbed of. My eyes fell back to the still steaming liquid inside the tan ceramic mug my hands were hugging for warmth.

"You seem like you have lost someone too?" Jan noted with a raised eyebrow.

My chest stung at the inquiry. I didn't know if I wanted to indulge her in answering. I pursed my lips instead and just nodded.

"I'm sorry, um—" she paused. "My flutters! You know, I never did catch your name."

"Esmari," I said. It came out more coldly than I intended.

"Ah, Esmari. Lovely name, Esmari is." Jan nodded with satisfaction. "Well, now, Esmari. I'm sorry you have had to experience a loss at such a young age. From the way you look, you two were close?"

Again, I nodded. "Yes. Best friends."

"Esmari, I take it that this is not the only thing that is troubling you lately. A loss is quite something to experience. Quite something to process. But it's more than that." She talked as if she knew everything about me. Something about her deductions reminded me of someone else, I just couldn't quite figure out who it was.

I took another long slurp of my tea and remained quiet. She didn't seem to be asking me for an answer, anyway.

"Are you heading anywhere in particular?" Jan asked. I found her voice comforting to continue to hear.

"I don't even know where I am," I mumbled.

"Traveling, without a destination? In this storm of ours? You really must be processing quite a bit!" Jan shook her head with a laughing sigh. "What District is your family from?"

"I don't have family here." *I don't belong here.*

"Ah," Jan breathed with understanding, as if I had just told her my whole life story in one sentence.

A wave of uncertainty washed over me as I glanced at the clock on the wall chiming nine. All I thought about was running away, but I didn't know where to run to. I wanted to disappear. I wanted to go somewhere I wasn't known. More importantly, somewhere that didn't remind me of Hunter for a bit. Somewhere we hadn't made memories together. Just long enough to process and figure myself out without the constant reminders of the lurking creep named Byrein. Long enough that I had time to breathe without the fear of hurting people who I knew. I guess being lost was the best way of disappearing.

"What are you thinking about now?" Jan questioned, her voice breaking me out of my thoughts.

I peered into the slowly swirling liquid in my

mug. Shrugging, I shook my head. "Just that I got what I wanted." *But at what expense?*

"Ah. Well, only time will tell if it was what you needed. Maybe being here is just what you need." She smiled.

I thought for a moment. "Where exactly is 'here?'"

"Oh, flutters me. You genuinely are lost, aren't you?" Jan chuckled. "Well, you are just inside of the border for North District. Judging by the cold outside, you likely were coming from West District."

"North District," I repeated.

"And judging by how young you look, you likely are still a student over at the academy, yes?" Jan asked.

"Yeah." I nodded.

There was a comfortable pause as we listened to the sounds around us. I found myself counting the tics of the second hand of the clock on the nearby wall.

"Do you have a place to stay tonight, Esmari?" Jan asked as she drank the last swig of her now-cooled drink.

Embarrassed, I shook my head. *The storm's too*

bad for me to find my way back to the dorms. But you hadn't planned ahead for the night when you left Jewel. Nice one, Es.

"Well, something tells me that I can trust you. I tend to trust my instincts on that. And you certainly need a place to just hide away while you process whatever it is that you are going through. It seems to be quite a doozy," Jan said. "I have a little apartment out back of my house. It isn't much. My grandson sometimes stays there when he comes to visit, but you are welcome to call it home while you figure things out."

She certainly is observant. I looked at her kind eyes. A feeling of safety and opportunity rose from deep down in my gut. Something told me that I could trust her, too. *What other choice did I have?*

seven

It was late when we arrive at Jan's home, and the snow was still coming down heavily outside. She showed me around back of her massive home. Part of me wondered what she did for a living that she could afford to live at such a grand estate. Or maybe what her late husband once did for work.

The stonework of the walls for the front house was beautiful in the accents of lamplight, and the snow swaying around it made you think that you were looking at a fake picture in all its perfection. It was mesmerizing, and at the same time, made me feel severely insignificant to be standing on the property. The squeal of the wrought iron gate's cold hinges echoed in the silence of the night.

Jan led us along a shrub-surrounded walkway, completely blanketed in white. Our shoes crunched against the icy path below our feet, and soon we were upon a small, cottage-like building. Jan reached down into one of the potted plants by our feet and retrieved a small, vintage key.

A breeze blew flurries of snow around us as she quickly wiped the key free of soil, before inserting it into the lock. A click of the brass doorknob sounded as she twisted it to enter the door.

"Brrr!" Jan giggled as she swatted off the snow from her sleeves.

I closed the door behind me just as another gusty breeze threatened us with a howl. Carefully, I stamped the snow from my shoes on the mat just inside the door. Jan found the light switch and flicked it on, allowing the warm glow to flood the space.

"Now, I know it's not much," Jan started,

taking a glance around the room before her. "There's a bathroom over that way, and you should find some toiletries that you may need in the cabinet, and that other door is the bedroom. The bedding is all fresh. And of course, this here is the kitchenette and living space. You're welcome to use the kitchen as you see fit, but feel free to join me for meals as well," Jan explained as she motioned along with her hands.

"Are you sure it's alright for me to stay?" I asked sheepishly. I suddenly felt like I was imposing on her.

"Oh, my flutters. Of course, it's alright! In fact, I am quite happy to have a visitor!" Jan chuckled as she shook her head. She went to the thermostat and turned the heat on. A moment later, we could hear the whooshing of warm air coming through the vents at the ceiling.

I looked around the space before me, feeling once again out of place. The decorations were simple and sophisticated all at once. There was such a coziness to the room with all the warm colors in the furniture and decor. The leathers and brass accents gleamed in the warm glow from the lights lit up all around the room. A shiny dark wood floor showed no footprints as if it had just been mopped.

"I will leave you to get settled. I have breakfast at about eight in the sunroom. Head straight for the house and take a right. Look for large glass doors, you can't miss it." Jan smiled, setting the key on the glass coffee table by the brown-leathered sofa.

"Thank you." I smiled back at her as she reached for the door.

"Make yourself comfortable, Esmari. Have a good rest, and I hope to see you at breakfast." Jan nodded goodbye to me and closed the door behind her.

I turned back to the space ahead of me and allowed myself to take a breath. My arms began to ache, but not from the cold this time. I knew it was my power itching to surface. *Okay, you win.*

I flicked a small puff of Energy to my finger as I wandered to the bedroom to ease the ache. The glow from the wisp on my fingertips was like a personal torch as I entered into the shadows. I carefully released more Energy and created a small ball of light, holding it at my fingertips. Mesmerized, I watched as the colors danced with the shadows against the walls. I could feel my wings filling out at my back as the glow around me increased. To my surprise, I didn't feel afraid.

Hunter entered my thoughts. His laugh. His eyes. His childishness. *He would have loved to see this.* My chest ached for him. I longed to have him sitting by my side as I learned and explored. To listen to him talking about carpentry. I wanted to be wing racing him through the sky. Or sitting up in the loft of the Dripping Crown coffee shop, sharing a sandwich and just enjoying each other's company.

Sorrow swirled inside my chest as I sat and stared at the ball of light on my fingertips. And it was at that moment, I realized I had no more tears left in me.

———

Early the next morning, I woke up to the gentle kiss of the sun creeping in from the window across the room. I crawled out of bed and placed my bare feet on the cool wooden floor. Memories from the previous day crept out of my head. Slowly, I took a breath and willed them away. The clock on the wall read fifteen past seven.

I wandered across the room to find where I had left my socks and shoes from the night before and slid back into them. Something about the serenity in the air made me feel secluded and at peace from everything. A sharp pressure in the back of my neck presented itself suddenly.

"Okay, I know," I spoke softly to my Mind Sight.

Compliantly, I sat on the ground and pressed a finger to the foundation beneath me. The whistling from the air vent faded from my hearing, and I closed my eyes as I pushed a surge of power from my fingertip.

A scene came into view in my head. Branches from nearby trees were weighed down by the heavy blanket of snow. A familiar figure came to view. Jewel stood wrapped in a thick sweater, looking out into the distance. "Es, I'm sorry. I just hope you're safe," she whispered. Someone stood beside her. Her dad, I think. It was too blurry to tell. "Just give her time," they cooed.

My surroundings returned, and I sighed at the episode. Even here, I am not alone. It was almost silly of me to think I could completely run away.

"I'm safe, Jewel," I whispered.

I sat for a moment, enjoying the cool ground against my bare ankle bones that peaked out from beneath my pantlegs. My mind wandered back to the moment it all started. The moment things began to unravel. Back to the pile of rubble that once resembled a home. Back to seeing the moment Hunter died. I allowed myself to feel. I didn't want to block it out this morning.

I remembered my anger that day. My terror. I recalled the moment I nearly killed a man. I wanted to know how I connected my powers, using my Energy during a Sight episode, if that was what I really did.

I replayed the feeling rushing through me as I sought out the Ex with my Mind Sight, as I pulled the Ex from the sky. I ran it in my head, over and over, analyzing it piece by piece, moment by moment.

I pressed my fingers into the ground before me once more and thought of the apartment home I was in. I released a jolt of power willingly, sending myself into another Sight episode.

I could see a flower sitting in a vase on the bathroom counter. It danced subtly as the air from the vent touched its petals. A single petal detached itself, ready to fall to its death. I willed myself to it. I pushed myself to reach for it. Instead, my surroundings faded back into view.

I stretched my neck and stood up as the grandfather clock out in the living room chimed seven forty-five. It felt odd to be so completely alone in such a large place.

I mulled over the conversation I had with Jan the night before. Her confidence in celebrating her husband's life well-lived was something I found myself longing to do about Hunter's life. He never liked to see people sad for long. Maybe Jewel was right. Maybe he would be disappointed to see me now.

I moseyed my way out the front door of the apartment home. Locking the door behind me, I tucked the small, sturdy key into my pocket. The gardens before me were even more magical in the morning light. A glittering blanket of white lay gently over the trees and shrubs to the sides of the winding pathway.

I felt as if I were ruining the perfection of the environment as I walked through the untouched powder. Though I could see my breath before me, the air didn't seem all that cold, and I found myself mystified as I wandered my way through the enchanting scene. A sense of adventure and hope rose within me, something I had long forgotten I was capable of feeling.

When I made it to the very glass doors Jan had told me about, she was already sitting at a table just inside. Pausing for a moment, I admired her well-put-together look, complete with glittering, grand jewelry and bright-colored attire. Her eye caught mine, and she waved me in happily. The door squeaked open from the moisture on its seal as I entered. Swiftly, I swiped my feet at the doormat to rid of the melted snow on my shoes and joined her at the glass table.

"Good morning, Esmari," Jan said with a chipper tone. "You look like you slept well."

I glanced at the fancy plate in front of me. There was a grand bouquet of wildflowers sitting in the center of the large table that smelled sweet and complimented the aroma of the danishes on a silver serving platter just below.

"Yes, thank you," I answered.

"Well, please help yourself. The danishes are freshly baked by my cook and still warm, might I add." Jan smiled.

She has her own cook? "Thank you," I mumbled again. With a pair of long tongs, I reached for what looked like a berry danish of some sort. The goopy frosting stuck to the tongs as I placed it on my plate. I replaced the tongs to their place on the tray with a clatter and winced. *Nice going, Es.*

Jan didn't pay any attention to it. "Do you want any juice or milk to go along with?" she asked as she pulled apart her danish with her fingertips.

"No, thank you."

"Well, if you change your mind, you're welcome to whatever you want." Jan nodded as she continued to dissect her danish. She pulled the sides from the cherry-filled center and nibbled at them first with her manicured nails.

I took my fork and tried to daintily cut small pieces off to eat. Feeling clumsy and awkward, I gave in, picked it up with my hands, and brought it to my lips for a bite. The mixed berry filling was just the right amount of tart against my watering tastebuds.

"So, have you ever been to the North District's outdoor market?" Jan asked casually.

"I've never been to anywhere in North District, actually," I noted.

"Oh, well, you just must go. It's got all sorts of goodies. A great place to get lost and quite possibly get found." Jan gave out a boisterous laugh. Her blush on her cheeks sparkled in the light of the morning. "Not too far from here, either. When you leave here, go right and fly until you see it."

"Okay, I think I will check it out." I nodded with a smile.

"Be sure to take time to see the indoor shops just past the market, too. There are lots of hidden gems there, in my opinion." Jan ate the last bite of her danish, and relaxed back in her chair, wiping her hands on a napkin.

I finished my danish as well and sat for a moment, satisfied with the flavor lingering in my mouth. I cleaned my fingers as best I could. A smiling woman in all-black attire and hair slicked back came in. She set a white plate with steaming towels on the table between the two of us. Quietly, she nodded to Jan and cleared her plate, then came to me and nodded to my plate as well.

"Yes, thank you, I'm done," I stammered uncomfortably. It felt too posh to be waited on like this.

The woman smiled again and took my plate

away. Jan took a towel and slid the plate closer to me to do the same. The towels were warm and moist. The steam was welcoming to my cool hands. I watched as Jan wiped her hands clean from breakfast, and I did the same. She and I placed the towels in front of us and enjoyed the silence of the morning together.

There was a subtle peace sitting in the sunroom that morning. I admired as Jan gazed out the glass, watching the world outside. I felt completely out of place in such a grand home, yet I felt blissful as I watched how such an outgoing and eccentric woman could sit in complete silence and just simply be in the moment. She looked as though she didn't have any worries to stress over. She wasn't thinking or pondering deeply. She was just observing the tranquility.

"Thank you for the breakfast," I said, finally standing from my chair.

"Of course. You can't process the difficulties of life on an empty stomach. You are welcome to join me again for lunch and dinner if you want to, but no obligation to. I encourage you to lose track of time and see what the day brings you. Something tells me that you may find some answers to questions you didn't even know you had." Jan smiled, looking at me slyly. "If you find yourself around, I have lunch around noon and dinner around five."

I smiled and looked her over. It was odd to have a complete stranger be so welcoming and kind. Again, I had an inkling prodding at the back of my mind. Something about her reminded me of someone else, but in such a discreet way that I couldn't quite place it. It was something in her eyes maybe, or the way she thought, yet the more I thought of it, the less I understood what it was.

"Thank you. I will see where the day takes me, I suppose," I said.

"Enjoy being lost!" Jan chuckled as she waved me goodbye, her bracelets laying over her sleeve glimmering in the light.

I smirked to myself and left out the glass door. Fluttering up into the clear blue sky, I headed toward the direction of the outdoor market Jan mentioned.

The air was crisp, but I found myself welcoming it like a hug from an old friend. My mind was at ease, more than it had been in days. The sense of being alone and a stranger to everyone was freeing. As I flew, I flicked puffs of Energy from the tips of my fingers like an old habit.

I thought of my wings. How they glow when I used my Energy. I wondered for a moment if it would change anything about my flight.

Suddenly giddy with excitement at the very idea, I held a puff of Energy between two fingers, the size of a blueberry. I could feel my wings extend behind me as I flapped high in the air. The sound shifted. The faltering rhythm of my uneven wings changed into a beautiful low whoosh with each flap.

A glow shone off of the snow on the rooftops as I passed, glittering a rainbow of colors. I found myself able to glide more steadily, without excessive flapping and fluttering from my uneven black wing portions.

Soon enough, I could see a commotion ahead from the outdoor market. *My glowing wings may draw too much attention.* I decided to land and walk my way in.

As I meandered, I found myself passing so many others who didn't so much as glance in my direction. Not a soul whispered about me as I passed. No one shot unsure glances at me as if I were a bomb that they expected an explosion from. No one cared who I was. And that feeling of being a nobody was something I didn't realize I craved as much as I did.

The commotion reminded me of my hometown. The way that there was such a bustle about the area. However, everywhere I glanced, there was such a high-end, classy presence. So much more refined than the people of Athra could even dream of being.

I passed by a couple of people's booths that were selling different types of produce, some I recognized and others I didn't. One man was already low on supply even though it was only just past nine-thirty or so. Another booth was selling hand-beaded scarves, but the woman didn't seem very approachable, though part of me was fearful of how expensive they were anyway.

The people around me were so diverse. They were of ages young and old. The beauty in the multitude of shapes and colors of wings surrounding me was more apparent in the beams of early sunlight. Royals and Non-Royals perused the booths around, all different tones of skin, all different backgrounds, all at peace, together in the high-end market. One thing they all seemed to have in common was their sophistication, their elegance. They all seemed wealthy, and not necessarily just in the terms of riches.

I wandered my way through the market, gandering at this and that. There was a plethora of people and booths with lots of fun things to look at. The heat lamps strewn about kept the place moderately free from the cool air. Every so often, I would walk a little slower past one of these heat lamps to warm up before walking through another cluster of booths.

I found myself drawn to one booth which had stones and jewelry of all kinds laying out along the tables. A woman next to me, who smelled of vanilla, purchased a beautiful purple stone strung on a cord to wear as a necklace. I admired how an iridescent stone changed colors in the light. *It's like the snow at first morning light.*

I smiled to myself, thinking of Jewel and me chucking snowballs at the tree outside our dorm building. Sadness began to cloud my thoughts as I longed to have had Hunter in that memory too. Instinctively, my fingers found my necklace, and I felt the small stone between my cool fingertips.

"Onyx. Beaut at that, might I say."

I looked up to see the man running the booth peering down at me. His height surprised me as he towered over me, observing my necklace.

"Sorry?" I said, pulling myself out of my memories.

"Your necklace, Miss." He motioned with a pudgy finger at my hand still lingering on the stone. "It's black onyx. Looks like, in its raw. Unpolished, that is."

I shrugged. "Oh, I didn't know."

"It suits you well. All stones are symbolic of different things, Miss. Black onyx symbolizes strength. You're a strong soul. I can see that. Been through something mighty, but strong because of your experiences," he explained. He stuck out his open hand at me. "May I see it?"

I thought for a moment, then nodded. Hesitantly, I took it off my neck and placed it in his hand. He looked the stone over gingerly in his rather large hands. I could see his passion for the stones in his eyes.

"The cracks in it are unique. As if there is more to this stone's story than meets the eye," he noted as he placed the necklace gently back into my hand.

"Never seen one like it. Never seen a stone so perfect for a person neither, Miss."

I smiled thoughtfully as I clasped the necklace back around my neck. "It was a gift."

"Mighty fine gift there, Miss. I'd say that stone chose you. That kind of fit between a stone and a person, that's rare to see."

Another customer approached the table and summoned him away. He excused himself with a quick nod and went to assist the new customer. I looked over a few more items at his table and noticed the man glance once or twice during his alternate transaction to snatch another look at the onyx stone on my neck.

I walked down the way where a woman was handing out samples of different types of homemade bread. Gratefully, I took one to nibble on as I continued my journey. The chatter from each of the table's vendors was like a low, comforting hum as I wandered. There was such variety in what each table had to offer, and yet they all seemed to begin to blend together in their ways.

The sun was high in the sky by the time I found my way through the maze of vendor's tables. A dull ache began to pester the back of my neck. I had been so lost in the wandering of the morning that I hardly noticed my need to use my powers.

A feeling of vulnerability grew inside me as I realized how crowded it was around me. The wind was picking up some as well, and I dreaded the thought of pressing my bare fingers to the cold, damp slush on the ground.

Mindlessly, I wandered down a small walkway toward what looked like small boutiques and shops. I gazed into a window as I passed, admiring a painter contemplating his work in a large, practically empty room. I continued on in a complete daze.

THUD!

Someone came around a corner and lost their footing in the slippery ice slush, sending us both to the ground. Muttering to himself, he yanked his beanie on his head and scrambled for the plastic folders that popped out of his now-unhinged briefcase. He stood shaking at the folders to get the excess muddy snow off of them and stuffed them violently in his briefcase.

"No, not today, why—my work—" he grumbled, frantically latching the locks of the case with a snap. The man pulled his beanie once again and tucked the still-dripping briefcase under his arm. With his head still low and eyes on the ground, he muttered a quick "sorry, ma'am," and was on his way.

I stood from the mound of muddy, slushy snow I landed in. Frustrated, I shook my arms and watched as clumps of ice slung from them. *Great. I'm sopping wet.* I attempted to swat the water from my pant legs, but it was no use. An unwelcomed breeze brushed past me and sent a shiver down my spine.

Wrapping my arms around me, I trudged on, listening to the sloshing sound against the souls of my shoes. It was quieter the further I got from the outdoor market. I passed by a trinket shop that had some low music coming from the slight crack in the door and smelled of flowers. A jingle from a door and a kind voice caught my attention. A woman was handing a customer her bags as she waved her goodbye at the doorway.

"See you next time!" she beckoned after her customer. Her eyes caught mine and she smiled. Suddenly, her expression turned to pity as she looked me over. "Are you alright?" she asked.

"Yeah, just, um, wet," I noted.

"Why don't you come in and warm up. Let's find you something dry to change into that's of your liking," she welcomed as she held the door for me.

The store inside had clothing and accessories all of the same cream color. There were several styles all over walls and racks throughout the small space. *Not much choice of color, but at least it's dry.* I took a look at the price tag on a nearby shirt. *And at least it's not too pricy either.* I sighed and began carefully picking through the different styles, looking for something new to wear. The woman disappeared behind a curtain to her stock room and returned a moment later with a towel for me.

"Here, dry off some, and I will help you look." She smiled. I nodded and took the towel from her outstretched arms.

We moseyed around the store, and she gathered a few pieces of clothing as I attempted to pat myself moderately dry. Every so often, she would get a shirt and hold it up to me, having a debate with herself whether it was the right style for my features, or the correct size to be comfortable.

She reminded me of Jewel in the way she held her confidence, but something about her tone of voice and her accent reminded me of Maya. Her wings flicked as she thought, revealing a copper smear on her left wing. *Wonder what her power is?*

The dull nagging sensation returned to the back of my neck. All of the commotion made me almost forget about it. I carefully took a breath and silenced the nagging a moment more.

"Alright, let's have you try these on and see how it fits." The woman led me to a small changing stall and hung the top and pants on a hook. "Take your time. Let me know how you like them."

I closed the long privacy curtain behind me and pealed my wet clothes from my skin. After struggling to un-cling the moist cloth from the wings at my back, I carefully dried off and tried on the outfit we had picked out.

The pants fit perfectly, and the oversized sweater was cozy and just what I needed. I looked myself over in the mirror and admired the trendy outfit on me. Aside from the odd cream color, it was perfect.

I pulled back the privacy curtain and stepped into the walkway with slightly damp socks, leaving a trail of wet footprints along the way. The woman came over and admired me like I was her work of art.

"What do you think?" she asked calmly.

"It fits well," I said.

"Good! You look great in this. Thought you might. Now, let's do something about the color!" she praised. The words were sweet to my ears as I looked over the odd-colored outfit once more.

I chuckled. "That would be great."

She stood next to me and peered into the mirror, cocking her head from side to side as she looked over the clothing. She admired my face for a moment. A slow smile formed on her lips. With the pad of a single finger, she touched the fabric delicately. Before our eyes, the pants changed to a deep, navy-blue jean color, and the sweater changed to a silvery gray. She looked it over again and shook her head as she tugged gently at the sweater. Again, she raised her finger and tapped the fabric on my shoulder. The silvery-gray rippled from existence and left a deep burgundy in its place.

"There. Now, how's that?" She smiled. I nodded, happy to see the fabric any other color than cream.

"Do you happen to have socks, too?" I inquired, shifting my increasingly colder feet.

"Oh, yes! Shoes, too?" she asked as she placed her hands on her hips.

"Yeah, I suppose so." I sighed, looking at the muddy tops of my shoes lying in a heap behind me.

She snagged a plastic shopping bag from behind her counter and handed it to me. "Why don't you collect your wet clothing and put it in here. I'll gather some footwear and put it over at the chairs for you." She nodded to a couple of chairs across the way.

I shoved my still-dripping clothes into the bag. Slipping off my damp socks, I placed them in the bag and stood barefoot on the cool tile flooring of the store.

Suddenly, I felt a surge of power leave my toes, and my surroundings fell away. I saw a small older man with a hunched back stacking books onto a table by a storefront window. His shaky hand slid across the front cover of the top book.

My surrounding returned to me, and the nagging in my neck stopped. I looked up at myself in the mirror and tried to put some understanding into what had just happened. *Sight episode? I can use my feet for that?*

eight

After I paid for my new outfit, I thanked the woman for her kindness and set out to find the bookstore with the old man from my Sight episode. I still didn't quite understand how I had brought on the episode with my feet, but what I did know was that I was drawn to finding out why. Why that man? Why that store? Why that book?

It didn't take long before I stumbled upon a similar window from what I remembered in my episode. A little wooden sign in the window read "open" and I found myself excited to explore. With my bag of still-wet clothing hanging from the crook of my elbow, I pushed at the heavy wooden door.

Nearly falling my way into the bookstore when the door gave way to the suctioned doorframe, I gathered myself and closed the door behind me. Looking around, I was grateful to see the store empty, aside from a lounging cat in the corner.

It was small and a bit stuffy inside, smelling of old leather and dust. I tucked my wings tighter against me as I slid past a table with a fragile-looking dusty lamp sitting by a high-backed velvet chair.

My eyes searched the space for the man I had seen. I heard shuffling of shoes against the wooden flooring and turned to see the man peering down at the book he was carrying through tiny wire-rimmed reading glasses perched at the end of his rather large nose. He sniffed and snapped the book shut before pulling the glasses from his nose and looking up.

"Hello!" I called. My voice boomed in the quiet space.

"Hello." The man's voice shook as he spoke. "Take a look around."

I headed right for the stack of books near the window that I had seen in my Sight episode. The top book still remained where I remembered it. There wasn't anything special about the cover, just a basic, warn fabric spine and dented corners of the hardcover. I carefully took it from the wobbly table it sat on and opened it up. Skimming the words, I flipped through the pages.

After some time of looking through its pages, and finding nothing of particular interest aside from a very small blurb on the history of Banshui, I set the book aside. A feeling of defeat entered my soul once again. *Why did I see this? What was the purpose? Was I reading too much into my Sight episode?*

I shook my head and allowed my eyes to wander the space of the shop. Dust and fibers danced in the rays of light coming from the window at my back. The more I gazed around the shop, the more I realized just how much larger the place seemed to be.

I took it upon myself to meander about the shop. The place reminded me of my Sight classroom but with so much more knowledge and history within its walls. There were rows upon rows of books.

Some golden-lettered books were all lined up on one shelf with the title *The Origin of Banshui* and then a volume number in a blocky font. There had to have been about thirty or so. I thumbed through a few of them before moving on.

The deeper into the store, the less light there was, making it hard to read some titles and find books. A couple of times, I would take a book from the shelf and tilt and twist it until the light would catch it just right, only to read the title and realize it was another book of no interest to me. *Unless you know what you're looking for, you may not have much luck, Es.*

My fingers and arms began to ache. Habitually, I flicked my finger by my side and puffed out a small spark of power to release the tension as I looked. Each puff provided a momentary brightness to some of the darker titles of the older books, making them less problematic to read.

I rounded the corner and continued down the next row of books. The old man stood at the other end, tilting his head back to see out of the thin reading glasses balanced on the end of his nose. He turned back and forth, his relaxed brown leather wings swaying as he resorted the books from the shelves. I continued on my stroll, getting lost in the adventure of titles before my eyes, and flicking puff after puff from my fingertips.

"Well, clip my wings and make me a crawler," breathed the man.

I glanced up to see him peering down the way at me. His hands lingering still on the book in his hands, with a page pinched between his crooked fingers. The man's eyes were wide with wonder and his jaw almost down to his hunched shoulders.

"Excuse me?" I responded finally.

"Do that again, young lady," the man requested in awe, waving a frail hand in my direction. "With your fingers. Do that again."

I looked down. *Did he mean my Energy power?* With a quick furrow of my brow, I lifted my hand and flicked my fingertips again, watching as the man's expression was one I couldn't quite figure out. "This?" I asked.

He nodded his head and slowly slid the glasses from his nose. Shoving the book from his hands onto a spot on the shelf, he kept his gaze toward me. I could see him searching for his words again, unable to piece together his thoughts. He shuffled his way over to me, and I found myself tucking my wings tighter and tighter to my back.

"In all my years," breathed the man.

I shifted my weight awkwardly. I wasn't sure what to think, either. But I had this anxious hope pressing in my chest. "Do you—" I stuttered. "I mean, have you— have you ever seen this before?"

"I thought the last of them had died out. Extinct. Gone. Never to be seen again. And then, to think, here in my shop! Yes, yes, here in my shop!" The man was beside himself. It was as if he were taking the whole moment in. He wrung his hands for a moment in thought. "What is your name?"

"Esmari," I answered. The man peered into my eyes, and I felt as though I was looking into his soul through his deep blue eyes. They were pure and honest.

"Esmari," the man repeated while nodding in satisfaction.

"Sir, do you know about this Energy power?" I asked cautiously.

"Energy power?" he questioned with confusion

clouding over his face. "I've never heard it called that before. Never heard that."

"Oh."

He turned away and shuffled down toward the front of the store. "Come with me," he welcomed, calling over his shoulder.

The man led us to the front of the store where he perused through a stack of books he had laying on the front counter by a beat-up-looking register. The cat, once lounging in the corner, came to say hello, purring as it weaved through our legs.

I watched quietly as the man continued, occasionally thumbing through a book, only to put it back and shake his head. He turned away from the stack with a perplexed look on his face. He shuffled past me to another stack of books near a short bookshelf and continued his search. The silence was awkward and uncomfortable, but I couldn't think of anything to say that would make it any better.

"Ah! Yes, yes," said the man, snatching a book swiftly from the middle of the stack.

The rest of the books rocked back and forth, and I watched, waiting to see them fall. Eventually, they slowed, and the man opened the book up, flipping through the tattered pages. He seemed to have found what he was looking for when a great big, crooked-teeth grin spread across his face.

"Here, take a look," he prompted, shoving the book at me.

I took the book from his shaking hands, and he turned away, shuffling toward the high-backed, velvet chair I saw when I first entered. He mumbled to himself, and he scooted his feet along. Slowly, he lowered himself into the chair with a hearty grunt, followed by a relieved sigh.

"The history of the Sage," I read aloud. My eyes darted back to the man who was slumped back in the chair.

He nodded smugly. "Yes, yes. Sage. Yes, yes. I came across this some time ago. It's a long-forgotten power. One of the original powers, back with the original Royals. Back when they wore fancy clothes and crowns."

"They used to wear crowns?" I asked.

"You certainly aren't a Banshui native, are you?" The man laughed.

"No, I grew up in Athra," I noted.

"Well, that explains that. Yes, yes, it explains that indeed..." The man's voice trailed off, and his gaze fell to the floor as if he were daydreaming.

"Sir?" I prompted. He had sparked so many questions in my mind.

"Yes?" he asked, seeming to snap out of his daze.

"Original powers?"

"Yes, yes. Original powers. There are a few. Deemed rarer. More important. Many have evolved. Many don't exist anymore." He shook his head in thought. "I've seen a few in my day die off. The last of the line. I've seen some be taken away and snuffed out like a flame..." His voice trailed off again.

Taken away? Was he being metaphorical? I couldn't quite tell with this man.

"Sage!" he announced quickly, snapping out of his daze once again. "True Sage. That's rare indeed."

"And what's a True Sage?" I inquired.

"A True Sage is something remarkable." The man's head bobbed up and down as he spoke. "Remarkable, yes, yes. Say, you ever heard of a Sight?"

"Yes."

"Well, there are special kinds of Sights who can

do incredible things. Yes, a True Sage is one of these."

"So, a True Sage is a Mixer? A Sage and a Sight?" I asked, trying to piece together everything.

"Mixer, that's such a silly new word you young kids use. But you can't be just mixing any two powers. Not any Sight, with any Sage. Each power has a complimentary power. And a person having both makes them a True..." The man's eyes drifted to the ground once again.

My mind swirled around the plethora of thoughts and questions. What type of Sight was he referring to? I wasn't even sure if I wanted to know. *Why had I not heard of any of this True business before?* I couldn't quite tell if the man was old and wise or just not quite all there. The man stared away with glossed over eyes as if he were completely lost inside of his own mind.

My gaze drifted back to the book in my palms. There was a sketch of a hand, not by the author of the book, but of a reader once upon a time. The sketch was of a hand holding what looked like a ball. Lines of what once were details of the drawing, were now just smudges, making it a blurry theory upon the pages.

I tilted the book from side to side, attempting to see their residual lines that were once there, the lines pressed darker than the others, hoping for a label or explanation. Unfortunately, the faded sketch provided no additional information.

I glanced over the words on the pages feeling engulfed by the growing length of the silence between the man and me. My mind was tired and overwhelmed, and I found it hard to focus long enough to actually read and comprehend the information presented before me. My eyes searched for the word "True" anywhere on the page and fell short. Somewhere on the pages, I read the words:

— described as feeling the power through the veins. Much like the feeling of electricity —

It baffled me how easily I could understand, how easily I could feel the words I was reading. For the first time, they didn't feel like foreign words. It wasn't an odd concept I had to master, but rather, much like a narration of my own being. It was describing me. What was in me. What power grew stronger and stronger by the day.

I flipped through the few pages about a Sage,

grasping, hoping for more information. I skimmed through the information. The mentioning of a long-lost Sage. The sentences about great power. Destructive and beautiful. It was hard to make sense of it all.

"It's getting late!" announced the man once again, nearly jumping out of his seat. "Yes, it's getting late."

I thought for a moment and glanced through the words on the page once again. Taking a breath, I asked carefully, "Sir, what kind of Sight is the compliment of a Sage?"

"There are these Sights called Mind Sights. Yes, yes, a Mind Sight power and a Sage power. A person who has both. That's a True Sage. Mind Sights are remarkable." He stood and shuffled in my direction.

"You sound as if you know one," I noted.

"I do indeed. Don't you? You seem like you are of age to go to the academy. Maybe you know him too." He gently took the book from my hands in such a way I didn't dare to ask for it any longer. "I think it's closing time. Yes, closing time. Very late. My dear will not be happy if I am late again."

I glanced out the window for a moment. "I'm

sorry to have kept you," I said softly.

"You had better get home too. Before it gets too dark out there. Your parents will be worried, young lady."

"Sir, my parents aren't—" I started.

The man was just shuffling away. He gave a quick scratch to the cat, who was now perched on one of the stacks of books. The cat purred and adjusted itself on the swaying stack below.

"I wonder what is for supper tonight. Better close up shop. Yes, yes. Close up. My dear will be mad at the books if I am home late for supper again," the man rambled on. He glanced over his shoulder, seeming in a slight daze again. "Say, I'm sure he is already spying on me, but if you see my Destimov out there, tell him that it's time for supper."

He turned back and shuffled away, leaving me alone with the dusty books and the cat.

nine

It was fairly late in the afternoon, and the chill of the slowly fading sunshine was beginning to set in by the time I decided to head back to Jan's house. Though I had snacked on a few things from different vendors and bakeries, I was finding myself famished, and ready for a decent meal.

I had so many new questions that the day had brought forth in my mind, but at the same time, such a peace with the amount of knowledge and experiences I had encountered through my day.

After I left the bookshop, I found myself unsettled, however. On the one hand, I wanted more than anything to go back again. I wanted to know what the man knew about me, about my power, about being a so-called True Sage.

But, his connection to the leader of the Exes also made me want to avoid the place at all costs. Initially, I thought the man to be a bit off, and I found myself questioning everything he said after I left.

If he hadn't remembered that Destimov was no longer, then how much of the rest of what he had said was something that I could trust to be true. Even still, there was no mistaking the recognition in his eyes of my power when he had first observed it.

I arrived back at the house a few minutes before five and was greeted by a chipper-looking Jan, who looked to be coming back from a stroll in the snow. The toes of her boots were covered in snow, and I watched as she clicked them together, allowing the little chunks of snow and ice to crumble off. She came to greet me in the front yard, already beginning to unravel her silk scarf from her neck.

"How was getting lost?" she inquired casually.

"Eventful," I noted, thinking once again over the events of the day.

"Well, you are just in time to join me for dinner," she invited, though I didn't think she was offering much of a choice. At the sound of my growling stomach, I happily obliged. Glancing back at me, she gave me a look that reminded me of someone once again, though I still had yet to figure out just who it was.

We entered through the large glass doors around back into her sunroom, and Jan peeled off her coat and gloves, tossing them at a nearby chair. She and I both stamped off our shoes on an elegantly designed doormat just inside the sunroom.

I set my bag of still-wet clothing off to the side of the room, near the doors, hoping not to forget it when I turned in for the night. By the time I looked up, Jan had disappeared around the corner, leaving me in a large, echoing, empty room.

I took the opportunity to gaze out the window at the fiery red glow of the sunset, bouncing off the snow on the ground, and making the freshly falling snowflakes look like ash floating from the sky. It reminded me of the explosion, and of Hunter, and of his death.

But, for some unknown reason, the memory didn't sting in my chest this time around. Instead, Hunter's face stuck in my mind and brought an unintentional smile to the corner of my lips. A shiver danced through me, and I hugged my arms to my chest, listening for any sign of Jan rejoining me.

Moments later, how many moments, I'm not sure, I heard the clacking of shoes echoing into the room. *That doesn't sound like Jan.*

"Gran?" called a voice. It was familiar to my ears.

The world slowed down as I began to realize just how familiar the voice sounded. I cringed at the thought. *Maybe you're wrong, Es. It couldn't be someone you know. You are just paranoid.*

"Gran!" beckoned the voice once more. I was sure of it this time. It was smooth and cut through the silence like a knife cuts through butter. *I know that voice.*

I turned to verify my suspicions. Rounding the corner was a tall individual with dark hair and defined features I couldn't forget if I wanted to. Kasius's black eyes met mine and softened with recognition. A mixture of grief and peace washed over me. The familiar sight of someone I knew so very far away from the school was causing a conflict inside me. *You just can't escape, Es.*

"You look unhappy to see me," Kasius noted calmly. *He really doesn't miss a thing, does he?*

"It's not you, it's—" I searched for the words to say that wouldn't come across incorrectly.

He nodded for a moment and smiled. "So, you met my, Gran."

"Jan? She's your grandmother?" I mentioned still piecing it together. He smirked with a nod, tucking a hand in the pocket of his charcoal gray slacks. *No wonder she seemed familiar to me.*

The woman from this morning, dressed in all black entered the room with a cart of food. She nodded a silent greeting of hello to the two of us, and continued to the table, beginning to unload the contents of the cart.

We watched in a blanket of silence as she set everything very strategically on the table and set a place for three people to dine. Just as quietly as she came, she exited the room.

I stared at the red tile flooring beneath my feet, searching for the words to say to him. I wanted to crumple to the floor. Guilt built up inside of me. Part of me didn't want him here. I didn't want to know anyone here. I liked the idea of blending in like a droplet of rain during a storm. I liked not feeling guilt or terror of hurting anyone in my life. I liked being lost.

"You changed your hair," Kasius casually mentioned. It wasn't a question, but I was beginning to realize he intended it that way.

I looked up to catch him gazing back at me. For a moment, I found myself slipping away into his kind and trusting eyes. Sheepishly, I looked away.

A clacking of Jan's heels beckoned in the room as she reentered. She looked just as spry as ever. Her eyes lit up with happiness at the sight of her grandson.

"Well, would you just flitter my flutters! This is a surprise!" she exclaimed, shoving her hands against her hips. She eyed me for a moment and then looked again at her grandson's face. "I take it we know each other."

I glanced back at Kasius's face, unsure how to

answer. Kasius smiled at her, hand still in his pocket, and nodded gently.

"Hello, Gran," he greeted.

"Don't just stand there, come on over and give your old Gran a hug!" Jan insisted.

He wrapped her in a large bear hug. His gestures toward her were so warm and loving. Almost as if he were a different person. Not as cold. Not as quiet. But yet, still just as swift and rigid as he usually was. I stood awkwardly, observing their encounter, feeling once again out of place.

"Are you staying?" Jan asked him.

"Yes, the academy is closed down while they fix some pipes. Looks like it will be a few days at least. I couldn't find the key to the apartment out back," Kasius explained. He nodded to me. "Now I know why that is."

Good job, Es. You took his home. "I'm sorry, I didn't, I mean, I can—" I struggled to get a plan in words.

Jan waved a decorated hand in my direction as if to hush me. "Kasius, you can take one of the spare rooms inside while you are here." Without waiting for an answer from either of us, she turned and headed straight for the table before looking down again at her hands. "Oh, flutters me. I still have something on my hands. I washed them twice already! I'll be right back."

Jan scurried out of the room, ticking her tongue as she examined the palms of her hands. I gave a silent chuckle and wandered over to a wall where pictures hung. I could feel Kasius follow me, but I didn't dare glance at him. There were just a few photos, mainly family portraits, hanging in beautiful wire frames. One with a young Kasius in it caught my eye.

"My parents," Kasius noted, his breath making a few strands of my hair dance against my cheek.

I admired their attire. He was positioned between them in a button-down shirt, as usual. They stood studious and proud in elaborately embroidered uniforms.

"They were a part of the ORP," Kasius said, nodding at the picture. There was an undertone of sadness staining the word "were."

"What happened?" I asked cautiously, though I didn't think I wanted to know the reality of the answer which was coming my way.

"They were a part of the raid against Destimov

and his followers. Part of the frontline of that raid. They didn't come home." His words stung against my ears, but his eyes wore pride.

I looked once more at the picture before nodding to an empty space where a nail sat without a frame hanging on it. "Is there a picture missing?"

Kasius nodded. "I have an older sister. Well, half-sister, named Renae. Her picture used to hang there. She left Banshui to be Destimov's follower, an Ex. Gran likes to pretend that I don't know the real story. She took down all her pictures, hoping we would, or I would, forget about her."

Kasius stared thoughtfully at the picture wall. I looked him over, piecing together his past. *There's so much more to him than he likes to let on.* It baffled me, his composure about all of it. Part of me wondered if he always was this composed, or if it was something that developed after all this happened to him.

His dark eyes fluttered to mine, holding my gaze. He stood quiet and intense. I could feel my heart beat faster, and my breath catch ever so slightly. It was as if he were trying to figure out my secrets, and I his.

"Come on, let's have some dinner!" Jan announced as she rejoined us.

Kasius flicked a smile at me and smoothly turned to walk to the table. He went and pulled the chair out for his Gran and helped her get seated. I quickly gathered myself, feeling flushed, before I took the same seat as I had that morning for breakfast and Kasius sat in-between us.

Jan chatted away, telling Kasius this thing and that. She talked about the house and the upgrades she had finished since he was last there. She talked about the weather and her new coat she had gotten to keep herself warm. She noted about going to the Redd's to celebrate her husband, just as she always did. Kasius would nod and listen. Every so often, he would offer a comment or two, which would send her into another topic.

It was well after we had finished our desserts that I finally found a moment to excuse myself from the table and head back to the apartment.

"Oh, flutters me. I just kept rambling, I'm sure that you both are exhausted from the day," Jan noted.

"Thank you for the dinner, Jan," I said, standing and heading for the door.

Her chatter with Kasius left me to my thoughts most of the dinner, and I found myself willingly lost in them, yet again, as I continued through the snowy path back to the quaint apartment home. I didn't feel overwhelmed with my thoughts exactly, more at peace to be able to think through it all. When I had made it to the door, the nagging of my Mind Sight was something I wasn't afraid of, but rather embraced.

I stepped into the warmth of the room and flicked on a light, closing the door behind me. I looked at both my hands and fingers and then at my feet for a moment. *I wonder if I could use my feet again, like I did back in the shop.*

Smiling as I assured myself that I was alone in the empty apartment home, I slid out of my shoes and slipped off one sock. With a deep breath, I placed a bare foot against the cold flooring, and willingly released a surge of power from the pads of my toes.

I could see a person with their back to me. They were sitting in a chair. A crossed leg bounced up and down in a rhythmic pattern. A shadowed hand held a metal cup, swirling the remainder of the liquid around inside. It was so quiet. I didn't feel afraid. I didn't feel anxious to know why I was there. I just was peacefully present. The man breathed calmly.

He took a hand and ran it against his short brown hair. I could see the tips of his black, crow-like wings sticking out from the back of the chair he sat in. I recognized him, yet I wasn't scared. Not even concerned. He looked peaceful. Thinking, observing his surroundings alongside me. A waft of air blew past the two of us, suspended in that moment. He turned slightly, revealing his scar along his jawline.

"Hello, Esmari," Byrein said. "I can feel you watching. Peaceful night tonight, isn't it?" He swirled the liquid of his cup once again. I wanted to reach out. I felt my hand lift up. Another breeze blew by and toyed with a rogue leaf as it fluttered past me. Byrein lifted the cup to his lips and then took a swig of it before he faded from my view.

My surroundings came back to me. My knees were stiff from standing still for however long I had been there. I instinctually found my necklace charm between my fingers and slid it along the silver chain, feeling as the eye rose and fell on each link. I wasn't scared to be in Byrein's presence. I wasn't uncomfortable. And I didn't know what rattled me more, the fact that I wasn't scared, or the fact that he knew I was there with him, unintentionally spying on his moment.

A muffled sound came from somewhere in the room, making my senses perk up. As if by second nature, I quickly flicked a puff of power onto my fingertips down at my side and scanned the room for movement.

A quiet huff of a smirk left Kasius's lips as his black eyes caught mine. He was relaxed back in a chair with hands folded casually, his legs crossed. I let out a sigh calming my nerves and snuffing out the spark of power at my fingers.

"Why didn't you say something?" I scoffed.

He glanced at my now-sparkless, fingers and back at my face. "I didn't want to startle you. You would've used it."

I looked at my hands and then at my single bare foot on the still cool flooring. *How long had he been there? How long was I standing there?* I don't want the answer.

"Why—" I started as I slid my other foot out of its sock.

He nodded to a plastic bag set against the wall.

Oops. Forgot to grab my clothes before I left. I smiled and nodded back a silent thank you.

"The door wasn't closed all the way. It opened when I knocked on it. I saw you inside standing there and not answering, so I stayed to make sure you were okay," Kasius recalled. It surprised me how thoroughly he explained himself. It felt out of character for him. Although, a lot of things surprised me today.

"Right," I breathed.

Kasius kept his gaze on me. He analyzed me, watching as I stood awkwardly, not sure what to say. Though his eyes were soft, it felt like they were burning a hole in my face. Patiently he waited. Waited for me to say something. Waited for me to move somewhere. To do something more than I was inevitably doing right then and there.

Something inside me made me want to be back in my Sight episode. I wanted to be back in that moment of peace next to Byrein, instead of standing here uncomfortable, unsure what to say or do, and shoeless.

Kasius was not making it any better with his intense staring. It made me uneasy thinking about all of it. I was confused. My gut twisted itself into knots, and I struggled to keep a grip on the moment. I stared back down at my toes, feeling the coolness seeping up my pant legs from the ground. I felt out of place. I just wanted to escape.

A familiar nagging pressed at my nape, and I suddenly found myself eager to let it in. Eager to launch myself into another Mind Sight episode. To be anywhere but here. And I didn't know why, nor did I so much as question the reason. My mind was muddled, and I needed some sort of clarity. It was as if I were being pulled in two different directions, to stay in this reality with Kasius, or give in to the nagging of my Mind Sight. The Mind Sight conquered just as abruptly as it presented itself.

With a surge from my toes, pressed firmly into the ground, I escaped into the episode. I couldn't see much. It was gloomy. But I knew the presence. I knew the feeling of the person who was here with me. More than I was willing to admit that I did. I knew it was Byrein again. Like he had called me back in some way. He was there, in almost complete shadow. I could just barely see his figure. But this time, it was different.

This time, it wasn't clear. He wasn't aware I was there. It wasn't peaceful. It was strained and uneasy. And all I could do was watch.

"You and I are connected. More than you now know," his voice hissed into the nighttime air surrounding us.

He wasn't calm, and yet, not angry either. A sense of obsession tainted his words like a sickening aroma I couldn't shake.

"You are stronger than you are aware. You could be of so much use to me," he whispered as if saying it to the rim of the cup, just barely visible in the fading light.

The last of the shadows faded from view, and the room I stood in broke through, including a furrow-browed Kasius. He sat in the same spot I left him, observing me. I felt worn down and foggy-headed. He kept looking at me without saying a word. He didn't need to. His eyes asked all the questions for him.

"I was with *him*." It was the only thing I could think to say. I needed to explain. He deserved an explanation.

I could feel myself shaking, not from the cold, but from the fright and panic building inside me. Suddenly, I longed for someone to hold me. To make sure I wasn't just going to crumble to pieces.

I searched Kasius's expression, watching as it softened from the stern, clenched jaw to careful concern. I could see him deciding what his next action would be. Slowly, he unfolded his hands and stood from the chair. In a short few strides, he came to me. He glanced at my shoes beside me and my bare feet below.

With a quick flick of his finger, my socks and shoes slid to the side of the room. Gently, he took my wrist with his warm hand, led me to the couch, and sat me down. In one swift movement, as if he had rehearsed it, he snatched a throw blanket from the arm of the couch and wrapped my shoulders, allowing the fabric to settle on its own around me. It was exactly the thing I needed.

He stayed there for a moment, watching my face, and, I'm sure, sorting all the thoughts inside his head, never once considering saying any of them.

I found myself grateful for his silence, and thankful that of all people to run into out in North District, I ran into him. A friendly smile curled at the corner of his lips and I saw all of the thoughts once lingering behind his eye fade away. He brushed a stray piece of hair behind my ear.

"I really do like the hair," he noted.
And just like that, he left the apartment.

ten

I woke up the next morning, still in the same spot on the couch as Kasius had left me, and still wrapped up in that same blanket. I didn't even remember going to sleep.

The sun was lighting up a good majority of the room, and the heater was just kicking back on, blowing warmth into the space with a hushed, whooshing sound. I was stiff from the firm couch and solid sleep, which became increasingly more evident as I stood up and felt my muscles stretch out.

A swift knocking at the door made me jump as it echoed against the solid flooring. Quickly, I smoothed my messy hair down, scrunching my nose at the bag of likely still-wet clothing, sitting where it was left the night before. Taking a quick sigh, I opened the door to a smiling and wide awake Kasius.

"Good morning," I greeted.

He nodded a silent greeting back. "Gran requested you to join us for breakfast." His voice was comforting and warm in the morning air.

He took a moment to glance at my feet, and then back at my face with a slight smirk on the corner of his kind eyes.

"Right, I need shoes." I chuckled half to myself.

I tossed on my socks and shoes. After a quick yawn and smoothing my hair as best I could into a quick ponytail, we were on our way to breakfast through the chilly morning fog. It was mystifying and eerie, and some part of me actually liked the unsettling vibe it gave off. Like we were wrapped in a blurry cloth, vulnerable to the world and its surprises.

For a moment, it was as though I could feel each molecule of the fog, watching it swirl around us, and tease at the icy ground below our feet. I could feel my power in my veins begging to play with it. With the energy and movement of the fog around me, unlike I ever had before.

As we walked closer and closer to the house, the want, the begging, turned into a craving. I was hungry to discover my desire. I didn't want to brush it off. I didn't want to deny it. I wanted to discover it. I needed to. *It's why you got away in the first place, Es.*

"What is it?" Kasius asked as if he were reading my thoughts.

"I just—" I thought for a second. "There's something I want to try. I'm not sure what exactly, or why, but I want to try it."

Kasius looked at me with his kind eyes. With a curl of his lip, he nodded. Without a word, he continued on his way to the house.

I was almost relieved that he wouldn't object, and even happier that he didn't ask to stay. I watched for a moment more as the fog engulfed the shadow of my tall friend and found myself giddy and anxious with excitement.

I focused on the swirls around me, watching as they danced merrily. Each curl wafted around another, without a care in the world that in a mere hour or so, it would disappear from the day. I felt each fold of the fog, where it was thicker, where it was thinner. With a flick of my nails, I held a spark of my power, just barely larger than the head of a nail.

I closed my eyes and felt each droplet of misty fog as it brushed against my cheek, then felt it against my hand. My palm. My fingertip. It was as if it were an extension of the ground and an extension of life. It was full of passion and carelessness. Most of all, it was full of energy.

I don't know why. I don't think I really cared why. But, for some reason, I felt the need to extend my power, to use that energy from the fog and allow my power to dance alongside of it.

I released my pinprick of a spark into the fog and felt as it twirled and jumped like a miniature lightning storm. I wasn't afraid. Somehow, I knew that the spark I sent out to pirouette with its fog partner was not dangerous. Not for me. Not for Kasius. Not for anyone hiding in the blissful blanket of the morning.

Then it happened. I connected. I connected to the fog. Maybe through my Mind Sight. Maybe through my Sage power. I could feel what it felt. I could see where it was, where it wasn't. I felt the resistance of the nearby tree as it slid around its bark. It pushed against itself to fill in the bare branches of a nearby bush. Its molecules as they brushed by one another, suspended in the air. I felt it. *Its energy.*

I flicked off another spark. Elated, I felt as it jumped from one molecule to the next. I could feel everything. Another, I flicked off, this time tossing it from one waft to another. I watched the colors transform and disappear from sight. *Can I control the color?* I smirked to myself and tried.

I thought of the color lavender and threw out a spark in that color. *It worked.* I threw out another spark, this time burgundy like the tones in Kasius's hair when the light hit it. I threw out three sparks to match the color of Mom's icy blue eyes and watched as they fluttered away. I thought of Jewel and sent out sparks to match the red oranges of her hair. I watched as the last remaining spark disappeared, snuffed out by the very molecules it danced and played alongside of.

I giggled to myself. It was all I could think to do. Hunter's face seeped into my thoughts. The memory of seeing his jade wings for the first time was like a bitter tea, sweetened with the purest local honey. And I let it. I didn't want to go away. I wanted it to stay. I wanted him to stay.

All at once, I felt the fog engulfing the space before me and, without another thought, I sent out my Sage power, my very own energy, to each and every molecule of the fog stretching from where I stood to the glass doors of the sunroom, where Jan and Kasius were waiting on me for breakfast.

What was once that thick, blinding fog, now twinkled my power. Hundreds, no, maybe thousands, of little, glittering sparks. All suspended in time. As if someone held the second hand on the clock still and hoped for the world to stop in that moment forever. It was breathtaking. Bright. Mesmerizing. And I had made it that way. I made something beautiful.

Across the way, emerging from the glass doors, were Kasius and Jan. I looked at them just long enough to see Jan clasp her hands over her mouth in awe. For once, I wasn't embarrassed by what I had done. I wasn't dangerous. *This is a Sage. This is my Energy power. It's not one or the other. It's both. And I think I love it.*

I admired my power, the beauty surrounding me. I wanted to see the jade of Hunter's wings as vibrantly as the first day I saw it. I wanted to experience its beauty in front of me once more. And that's exactly what I did.

eleven

The next several days seemed to fly by as I enjoyed my freedom, and before I knew it, those days were beginning to turn their way into weeks. I found it increasingly more comfortable to go out and explore the area with the small number of people actually knowing me there.

The schools had opened back up over a week ago, but I had no desire to return, as of yet. I wasn't ready to face it all. I wasn't ready to go back to being the center of everyone's attention. And I was not ready to face Jewel. Not yet. Not with Byrein's words still weighing so heavily on my mind.

Kasius agreed to let Mr. Higgens know that I just needed time. Time to process. Time to learn. To which I was very grateful. Though, I found that I missed having his familiar face around all the time. His quiet thoughts and little to no judgment as I explored and adventured on my own for the first time in my entire life.

Jan was overly accommodating and even mentioned several times how it was nice to have another woman around. She never once made me feel as though I was overstaying or unwelcome. Quite the contrary, in fact, often noting that she hoped I'd stay a bit longer. Always greeting me with a chipper face and interested in what new experience I had encountered that day.

I had been discovering so much about not only myself but about Banshui itself. About its rich people here in North District, and also about its rich culture. The history of the place had so much to tell and so many secrets to hide. It was both mystifying and terrifying, and both left me wanting to know more. I wanted to understand this place, this part of the world that, up until less than a year ago, I had absolutely no idea existed.

I was beginning to realize what a mix of people populated this part of Banshui. So many wealthy people, who were seemingly rich for being rich. So many people living so grandly. Living like, well, like the kings and queens, like absolute Royalty. The kind I had only read about in fairy tales.

Then again, who was I kidding? I was living the life you only read about in a book. Filled with tragedy and heartbreak, and yet, so many unbelievable things, that I could hardly keep up myself.

However, the more I learned and explored, the more I realized how very little I would find out about myself. About my powers. About others, past or present, like me. It was as if what I was didn't quite exist. All except a few very vague mentions from a book here, or a person there, of the "ancient Sages," and never more. It was as if I was not supposed to exist the way I was. Not here. Not now. Not in this time.

The more I learned and experienced, the more I thought about the only man who was capable of giving me any sort of answers. The man from the book shop. The man somehow connected to Destimov, and by extension, Byrein. And I had finally gotten to the point where I wanted answers more than I cared about his connection. *I'm going back. I'm getting my answers.*

The sun was high in the sky, and it was evident that the snowstorms we had been experiencing lately were not nearly over. Not by a long shot. I flew today. I had been enjoying a stroll by foot most days, especially as I got into the bustle of the outdoor market. But today, I had a mission and a destination.

I arrived at the alley that I had visited all those weeks ago. It seemed like a lifetime ago. I strolled past the clothing boutique and waved a simple hello to the woman who worked there. She and I had become acquainted on several occasions during my stay here, all starting with the day she helped me dry off and get some clean clothes. In a way, I owed my knowledge of the bookshop, and further, the beginning of finding answers about my power, all to her and her little boutique. She greeted with a warm smile and waved back before giving the floor mat in her hands another firm whip and watching the last of the dust puff into the crisp winter air.

I felt my heart beginning to pound as I saw the door to the book shop in the distance. I couldn't describe the feeling I had inside of me as anything other than reserved hope. But as I began to take each step closer to the shop, my heart began to sink instead.

No, no, no! The shop was locked, and all lights were off. A small sign in the window read "closed." *How could this be? It's the middle of the day?* I tried at the door once more, even knowing it was locked. I wanted it to miraculously open, and the man in the shop to greet me in his peculiar way. Cupping my hands over my eyes, I peered through the dusty, smudged, freezing cold glass of the window, peering inside to have some glimmer of hope rekindle inside of me. It didn't.

"But I need answers!" I grumbled to myself.

"Not from that shop, you don't," said a woman.

"Excuse me?"

"That shop's closed. Been that way, young lady," said the woman. She was tall and beautiful and took me completely by surprise. Her slightly sharp voice didn't seem to match her in the least.

"What do you mean? When did it close?" I asked frantically.

"Oh, I can't remember the last time I saw the poor old fellow have his shop open. He's lost it a bit. You know, up here," she noted, tapping at her temple. "Sad to see, really. He was a nice man. Just had so many tragedies, one after another. Wasn't the same since. His knowledge and his books were a rarity."

"But I was just here. I spoke with him. He has answers that no one else did." I pieced it all together.

"Well, you were definitely one of the lucky few then! I pass by nearly every day, and haven't seen the poor fellow in years, not since— ah well," she ticked her tongue. "There's a book shop up the way, maybe you will have some luck with what you're looking for! It's called 'Binding Books' just around the corner there."

"Thank you, I was just there a couple of days ago," I sighed.

The woman looked at me with pity in her eyes. She took a glance at the "closed" sign on the window, then flashed me a sorrowful smile and waved goodbye.

The feeling of defeat with a tinge of betrayal crept inside of me. I yearned once again for answers, and once again, felt like I had a door slammed in my face, meeting yet another dead end. I wanted so eagerly to talk with someone, anyone who even remotely knew how it felt to be me.

A thought of Byrein flashed into my head, and for once I entertained the idea. I dwindled on the fact that he knew how it felt to be a Mind Sight. But it was more than that. He had answers.

I wasn't ready to just jump at that idea, though. Not yet, at least. I took one last look at the lightless bookshop and shoved my chilly hands into my pockets. I wandered for a while through the alleys and the streets. I watched as people were all over, living life so carelessly, it seemed.

It was hard to look anywhere without seeing someone, somewhere, using their power. It was something I didn't think I would ever grow accustomed to. No one was ashamed of their power. No one was trying to ever suppress their power, from the looks of it. It was like they all used it as an extension of their everyday lives, to complete everyday tasks. And yet, it felt like it was all such a waste.

They have abilities that people from my hometown could never dream of. To move water without touching it. To light a fire with a single breath. To manipulate metal as if it were a piece of string. I wondered for a moment if any of these people, these Royals, had ever stepped back and thought about how fortunate they were to be who they were. Had they ever thought about the potential they had inside of them? Had they explored the limits of their power? Had they even wanted to?

I found myself pondering the limits of everyone's powers around me. A woman passed by with a small flame cupped in her palms to keep her warm. *If she can manipulate fire, what could she do with ash? With heat itself? How useful could it be if you can create color, then you could also take it away? Color is the product of light. Without light, we couldn't see color. Can they manipulate light itself? Can someone who manipulates light and someone who can create color work together and cause those around them to perceive only what they want others to see? What if it were the same person? A Mixer who could? Everything around us has water, what would happen if they could learn to move and control more than just water and liquids but how it moves and how it's used in plants? In people?*

"No," I said, shaking myself out of my thoughts.

A shiver ran down my spine as I began to realize just how scary it was to think of all of this. But what was more terrifying, was that I could feel deep down inside me the energy surrounding me, and what it could produce. What all these Royals around me were accomplishing with their power, and what more they could accomplish. It was unsettling. It was empowering. And I didn't know which feeling was worse.

"Esmari!" rang a familiar voice. I turned to find Jan striding toward me with bright eyes and a smile that could brighten even the worst of days. "Oh, I thought I might find you here!"

I offered a quick smile and hid the dark ideas once lurking in my head.

"How would you like to go on a little adventure?" she offered.

Anything to get back to reality. "Sure, what do you have in mind?" I asked trying to sound hopeful and eager, but knowing very well that I was failing at it.

Jan didn't seem to pay my fake-chipper voice

any attention. "There's something I think you should see. Now, I have been trying to stay out of your way while you took your time to heal and process from whatever it is. But, well, flutters me, I think it's high time that I intervene. Even just this once."

I smiled at her, and unbeknownst to her, I was grateful for her timing. She led us away from the cluster of shops and chatted about this and that. Pretty soon, we were coming up on some high-end shops and business buildings, as well as some exquisite homes that made me feel inferior.

As she prattled away, I couldn't help but wonder what she was preparing to show me. I could feel my Sight nagging once again, and I attempted to silence the urge for a bit longer.

"Okay, so enough with the chit-chat. I'm going to get down to what it is I want you to see. And truthfully, it isn't anything in particular, but it's several things. Several things that I think you are missing. Now, you didn't grow up around these parts, which means that you didn't grow up knowing the true nature and true power around you," Jan noted. She turned to a couple of buildings and extended a quick finger in the direction of a tall, red-bricked building that looked very old. "That right there is the main building of the ORP. It used to be a place where the old-time Royals would gather and analyze the lands from all over. Making sure that villages and towns were playing nice with each other. Back when we had a ruling king and queen over this land."

"What happened to that?" I asked.

"Well, we still technically have a ruling family, of the same bloodline. Flutters me, I am getting a little ahead of myself if I explain that just yet. Calm your wings, we will get to that and you will see soon enough." She chuckled for a moment and gathered her thoughts again before continuing. "That ORP is equipped with Royals with some incredible power who are destined to do great things. They protect, not just Royals, but they also help protect the towns and villages should they need it."

"I see, so, places like Athra," I half breathed.

"Yes, places just like that. Now, you see those homes? Those are homes of people who either worked to get where they are, or they were born into it as a descendent of the courts from those old times we just mentioned, the ones with kings and queens all dressed in actual crowns and jewels and elaborate gowns." Jan's eyes glittered as she spoke of the histories of her homeland. "Actually, if you take a look just over that way, there is one of Kassius's, and your, classmate's home. Her name is Belleza. Her father is one of the Authoritative Elders. Quite the important role."

I pursed my lips together at the thought of Belleza, trying to hold my tongue. The home Jan motioned toward was an elaborate, white mansion, complete with ornate stained-glass windows and gold accents. *Of course, her home would be grand.*

"This is all so fascinating, but I don't understand what it has to do with me?" I asked. I didn't intend it to sound as sassy as it seemed to have come out.

"Esmari, do you think all these people are insignificant?" Jan asked abruptly. I looked around at the mansions around us and shook my head. "Well, how about powerless? Or do you think that they shy away from their power?"

Again, I shook my head. I didn't understand why she was asking this. It seemed out of place to learn about this from her.

"Many of these people, these families, are solid

crowns. They come from Royals and have a long line of Royals. They are powerful. They have abilities within them that they strive to protect and perfect," Jan explained. She took a sigh and began to stroll. Without a word, I followed.

I could see a beautiful castle suspended in the sky just ahead of us. From where we were, it was massive and grand in elegance and looked as though it had been around for ages. I couldn't help but let my gaze fall on it and observed what I thought looked like guards in a watchtower. From the corner of my eye, I saw Jan glance at me, and then follow my eyes to see what had caught my attention.

"We are Royals, but they are the true line of the ruling Royalty. Our ruling family of Banshui lives there. Yes, they still exist. They are of the same bloodline for as long as Banshui has existed. They oversee, well, everything that you see here. They approve of who does and does not become ORP. Who is an Authoritative Elder. They approve of defense tactics and anything to keep and protect not only Banshui but also to keep Royals safe. It's hard to explain really. But just know they are the ones who call the shots, so to speak. They are some of the most powerful and most pure lines of Royals." Jan paused finally and took a moment to consider her next words as she adjusted the large emerald ring on her finger. "These are some of the most dedicated people, the most dedicated Royals to their power."

I peeled my eyes from the mesmerizing sight of the castle. My throat closed slightly as I tried to swallow my anxiety back. Jan's eyes were kind but more serious than I was ready for.

"You see, I think something of you. And I may be wrong, but I often am not. I think you have all this power inside of you. I think that you have more power inside of you than you know what to do with. And what I have seen, I am sure that it is just the tip of the iceberg, so to speak. You have an ability that I have never seen, and something I am sure many folks didn't think existed," Jan said.

Ha! You think I don't know that for myself? I held my tongue and kept myself from being snarky toward her.

She continued. "But I think you are letting your fear of your own power, of the past, and of what you might become, I think you are letting all of this consume you. Now, I am aware that I don't know the whole story. But, at one time in Banshui's history, a Royal like you would have been sought after. You would have been a leader. Praised and maybe even given a role in court by this very ruling family. I have seen you on more than one occasion shy away from your power. From your ability. This Power is within you. It is a part of you. Just like it is a part of all these people around us."

I nodded, trying to focus on what she was saying. I wanted to understand. The nagging of my Sight returned and I hushed it once again, begging it for more time.

"You see your fear is something that can either make you great or turn you sour. It will twist you. It will cause you to turn for help in unsafe places. It will corrupt you. You have lost someone of great significance in your life. That much I know. A best friend of yours is now gone. You blame yourself. You are afraid of who you are becoming. You are afraid of becoming someone and growing without this person in your life. But maybe you shouldn't be afraid of that. Maybe you can grow. Don't forget them, but don't cling to their lack of presence so much that you spiral into ruin."

Her words hit me like a brick and I broke

down. I don't know why, but I wanted her to know. I wanted her to understand. I wanted someone to understand. "If it weren't for me, Hunter would still be alive," I said. "It's my fault. I brought him here. If I wasn't who I am, he'd still be here."

I felt as if all of the pressures of the world were crashing down on me. I could feel all the energy around me. It was like lightning. Like sharp electricity against my skin. I had gotten so far. I had been doing so well. I had been coping. His memory had stung a little less every day I was here.

Now, out of nowhere, this woman had triggered something in me. I couldn't explain it. I couldn't understand exactly why, but I was crying and overwhelmed.

"Your power, and suppressing your power, will hinder your ability to cope. It will feel like a weight on you. It will make you irritable at the smallest things. It will mess with your emotions. Your body isn't meant to keep it all inside and suppressed," Jan spoke calmly. She wasn't even fazed by my breakdown.

Gray clouds were covering the skies and taunting us with another storm. I wiped my tears from my chin with my sleeve and look up at Jan's hazel eyes. More and more the feeling of electricity prickled around me. It was as if I could feel the swaying of the plant nearby, and the humidity in the air as it brushed against the stone walkway. I could feel Jan's presence. Her power inside her, though I didn't know what it was. And most of all I could feel my own Sight pinching at my nape once again.

I took a breath and suddenly words fell out of my mouth. They pieced together what I felt as if I were telling myself, and not Jan. "I don't know how to become who I am supposed to be without Hunter. I brought him because I didn't want to be alone here. But he was attacked, he died because they wanted me. They wanted to trigger me. And I could only watch it happen. It was my power that made me sit and watch it unfold. We were supposed to keep each other safe, and I failed."

"So, you're the girl. You're the Sight," Jan breathed. "My flutters. But what I saw wasn't Sight."

"I'm a Mixer. I became one that day," I remarked coldly.

"You always were one, but that tragedy

brought it out of you faster than you were ready to control it. It's no wonder you needed to process things. No wonder you push your power away," Jan commented, almost to herself. She nodded and smiled with pity. "There's one more place I want to show you."

I followed her mindlessly down to the end of a row of elaborate houses, away from the castle of the ruling family. Soon, we rounded the corner and headed to a vast field with snow-and-ice-covered boulders lining the paths. At the far back, just above the ground, a small stone mansion floated, complete with towers and flags that looked as if it was abandoned. Untouched for years and frozen in time.

"Who do you think could have lived here once? What type of family found their home here?" Jan asked humbly.

I looked it over for another moment and listened to the quiet peaceful air surrounding us. "I assume someone who was important at one point. Someone who did great things in their lifetime."

Jan pursed her lips and folded her hands in front of her. "Someone powerful. This is the home of Destimov. This is where he began his planning.

Where he began his recruits for other Ex's until they were discovered and chased from Banshui. This is the home of someone of great power, who didn't choose the right path. He was a solid crown. With a line of Royals before him. He was someone who let his fears and his doubts control him. He came from the same town as so many other Royals. The same background and upbringing, if not a better one than so many others. Yet, his path was so, very different."

I was stunned. I could feel the energy of the place here too. The power it held. Somehow, it didn't feel bad. It didn't feel wrong. Just connected. In a way I couldn't describe. I felt a calling to me, and out of pure instinct, I placed my hand on the icy ground and answered.

In the most gentle way, I floated into a Mind Sight episode. I was completely aware of being in one, still connected to where my body remained, waiting for the episode to finish. I floated through the space. Suspended somewhere above Banshui, I saw people, all going about their days. I watched them use their powers. I felt the pressure release as each person executed some mundane tasks of the day, with one power or another. I could feel how it was all connected. I could feel how one power could link to another. How they could feed off of one another. I could feel something else too: the implication of there being so much more potential.

"Ahh, you see it? Don't you? The ability for more?" said Byrein's voice. But as if he weren't talking to me, just echoing through the moment alongside me.

I pushed his words from my head. I saw the potential for more, and I could feel something in me almost break. They had potential, and so did I. They have choices and are making them. And it was time I took charge and made my choice. I was not like Byrein and I never will be.

twelve

I never did explain to Jan what had happened with me at Destimov's home. She didn't ask. Though, even if she had asked, I'm not sure I would have known how to explain it all to her.

But what I think she was aware of is something in me changed, and if I wasn't mistaken, she was rather proud of herself over it. All of it made me curious just how she would have known. Just how did she come to the conclusion that I needed that excursion with her?

I couldn't quite explain it, but I felt completely different after our little adventure together. I was empowered by the feeling of everything. Allowing myself to truly experience the connections around me. Knowing the power people had surrounding me and knowing the choices made.

I think it made me understand my connection to Byrein as well. The connection between our power. After quite literally seeing it all in the Mind Sight episode. But I could feel a strain between us as well. The purity in connections between one power to the next seemed to be something even Byrein didn't quite understand in full. Specifically, the connection to me.

Jan and I were surprised at lunchtime a few days later by a familiar face to both of us. Kasius had returned for the afternoon. He looked happy today, though it was hard to tell under his face of stone. But I think there was a twinkle in his eye at the sight of his Gran.

Everything about the afternoon felt right. The chatter of Jan as she rambled on about whatever came to her mind, and her chuckle as she laughed at her own stories she had for Kasius. The air felt different as well that day, as the warmth of the sun broke through the clouds. The food was as flavorful as it was the first day I got my wings, an experience I didn't know I missed so much.

Once finished with her lunch, Jan excused herself from the table, saying she was meeting a friend that afternoon and needed to get ready, which left Kasius and me to our thoughts. He allowed his gaze to fall on me and remained quiet for some time.

My mind danced with what I should say to strike up a conversation with him and release us from the silence of the room. The woman dressed in all-black came by and nodded at us as she cleared our plates.

"Thank you," I offered. She didn't say a word, just smiled and walked from the room.

"She can't speak, you know," Kasius noted. His voice was soothing and floated with the tranquil afternoon air, but his words caught me off guard.

"What?" I breathed.

"Mrs. Jay. She can't hear, nor can she speak. She reads lips, though," Kasius clarified.

I shook my head and smirked to myself. "I

thought she just didn't like me all this time!"

Kasius curled the corner of his lip and looked down in a silent chuckle. He took a deep breath and then looked me over for a moment in thought. "Jewel keeps asking about you."

I had spent so long here that I had almost forgotten about what made me come in the first place. Her name stung against my ears as I began to realize I would have to face her again at some point. And it was becoming more clear that it was about time to get back to reality and return to the academy.

I nodded. "What have you told her?"

"Just that you needed time," he noted as he took another sip of coffee from his mug.

I nodded again. *You need to fix things with her, Es. You need to be brave and prepare yourself to face it all again.*

"You don't have to face it alone," Kasius assured.

Certainly, he's not reading my thoughts. "I think I want to go back to the academy."

Kasius nodded and I could see a hint of relief in his eyes before they flicked to his coffee mug resting between his hands. I thought of Hunter, again, and how this felt just as scary as the day I decided to come to Banshui. Scary and right. Like a bubbly mixture inside me. I thought of his wings, the tone of jade. Like a smooth, pure stone.

"Would you like to go somewhere with me?" I asked. "I want to make one last stop before heading back."

Kasius was peaceful in the moment and just smiled to accept the invitation. He tilted the white mug to his lips and drank the last drop of coffee, before standing and smoothing down his periwinkle-colored button-down shirt. I stood as well and we were on our way.

Once outside, I opened my wings to the afternoon air and took off with Kasius close by. The air tossed his hair gently, revealing the multitude of burgundy tones to match his outstretched wings behind him. He flew effortlessly with a stone expression on his face. My heart fluttered with the presence of a friend beside me today.

We made our way to the outdoor market and landed quietly on the ground before tucking our wings away and strolling toward the booths. We wandered with purpose today.

Kasius didn't ask what we were looking for,

but instead was just there to be with me. He walked with one hand tucked just into his pocket and the other swinging rhythmically at his side, keeping his steps in beat. My eyes caught the booth I was looking for, and my heart leaped with joy inside my chest.

I approached the booth of the man who sold the multitude of stones and watched as recognition swept his face.

"Black onyx. I remember you, Miss. The strong one." The man smiled. "Looking for something special, Miss?"

"Jade. Do you have any jade?" I asked eagerly.

The man hunched over and glanced through his stones laid out on the tables, passing them by with a pudgy outstretched finger. Anxiously, I flicked a look at Kasius beside me, who was perusing the stones himself.

I returned my gaze to the man with hopefulness lingering in my chest. He furrowed his eyebrows as he glanced across the stones, shaking his head every so often. Carefully, he brought a hand to his chin, to give it a quick scratch in thought, and then would look through another group of stones.

Suddenly, he snapped his fingers together in an "ah-ha!" moment and reached to pull out one of the boxes under the table. With caution, he slid one of his display trays aside and propped the box on the edge of the table. He reached in and gingerly retrieved a very small stone.

"Looks like this is all I've got at the moment, Miss." He offered out a hand with the stone in my direction, pity filling his eyes. "Sorry, I don't have more choices, but is this what you might be looking for?"

In his large hand, he held a tiny, perfectly round, perfectly smooth jade stone. The exact color of Hunter's wings. My heart skipped with delight and hurt with longing at its sight.

It was perfect.

———

It was early evening by the time Kasius and I had landed in front of the dorms. We had caught Jan at the edge of North District before leaving, allowing me the opportunity to thank her for all she had done and to say farewell. It felt odd leaving the peace of her home, and I knew I would miss her immensely. But feeling the path now below my feet and smelling the familiarity of the dorm courtyard reassured me of my decision to return.

I found myself fiddling with my necklace's new jade charm as it lay comfortably beside the onyx stone on the chain. It almost was odd to be here. Like it had been ages since I had last walked through the doors now standing before me.

Yet, for some reason, I felt like I was closing a chapter of my life and starting new, and in some way, felt stronger than ever. I can't quite explain it, except that it just felt right again to be here.

Kasius flashed me a dignified smirk and nodded his head to me, waiting for me to take the first step. Make the first move. He watched me and studied my body language, and I found myself once again grateful for his few words and strong presence. I took a breath and opened the doors.

It was quiet in the lobby of our dorms, just as peaceful as the world was outside on our flight over here. A little piece of me expected to see Belleza's face and was prepared for her to show up and ruin my homecoming. Kasius stepped inside after me and stamped the snow from his shoes. He shrugged off his coat and glanced once again at me.

"Do you want me to walk you up?" he offered.

I thought for a moment, and though it was a tempting offer, I shook my head and pressed my lips into a determined smile. "I think I need to see Jewel on my own."

A moment of pride flickered in his eyes, and he gave me a nod. He handed me the small tote containing a few pieces of clothing I had gathered during my stay in North District. For just a moment longer, he looked me over before draping his coat over the crook of his arm. He turned swiftly, tucking his free hand in his pocket, and strode off.

I found myself glancing around, observing every sound, every color, every detail surrounding me as I walked up the steps, closer and closer to my dorm, and Jewel's. Each step made nerves catch in my dry throat little by little. I wrung the strap of the tote draped over my shoulder and felt the warm air from a nearby vent as it wafted past my wings.

What am I going to say to her? Jewel, you were right. Jewel, I'm sorry. Jewel, I missed you. I shook my head. *Hi, Jewel, did you miss me? Too cocky. How about, Hi, Jewel I'm an awful and terrible excuse of a person. You can hate me. She will likely take you up on that one, Es.* I sighed to myself as I stepped up to Jewel's door. I raised my hand, ready to knock, and froze. *Come on, Es. You have to do this. You have to say something to her. You're going to knock. On the count of three. One…two…*

"Es!" Jewel's voice echoed in the hall. I looked up to see her overjoyed face, beaming with shock and excitement by the common area down the hallway.

She turned back and forth as if she didn't know what to do with herself. She half bounced a handful of times, before hurrying down to where I stood, hand still awkwardly suspended in the air. *Okay, here goes. At least she doesn't look angry.* I calmed my breathing and lowered my suddenly trembling hand.

"Es! Hi!" she greeted nervously. She looked like a small child, unsure if she was allowed to show her excitement. Like a kid who was just told to calm down. She was eager and unsure. More than I had ever seen her before. "You, uh, you look different, Es. Better different. In a good way, you know?"

I smiled at her. "Yeah, I feel different."

"You look really, really good, Es," she offered again. Her blue eyes glittered with satisfaction.

"Thanks." Words felt odd.

"I'm glad you are okay."

"I am. At least I'm getting there."

Jewel looked for a moment at her feet and fiddled with the hem on her shirt as if she were fighting back what she wanted to say. With a grunt, she gave up.

"Es! Do you know how worried I was? You were so—so—" frustration filled her voice. "Uh! And you just left. Like that! In the middle of a storm. Disappeared. After I brought you to my parent's. After everything. You just—just left! And you didn't even explain. And I didn't know where you went! And I didn't know if you were going to be okay! How could you do that? How could you just leave like that? How could you do that to me?"

Tears were streaming down her face. Tears of frustration. Tears of fear.

"I know—" I offered.

She gave me a hesitant shove on my arm and continued. "That was an awful thing to do. You were an awful friend for doing that—not that I think you are an awful friend because you came back—but still! I begged you to come back inside then. You know I get hot-headed and I say things I don't mean, but you just left. And—and— the stuff I said about Hunter—and—and—you just shut me out. You kept shutting me out. I kept trying to be patient—"

"You were right," I cooed.

"But you disappeared on me. I didn't know if you were okay. And you were mad. And I thought it was my fault— and—and dad said I should just give you time—" She paused, finally catching what I had just said. She smeared the tears from her chin. "What?"

"You were right. I was awful. I had a reason I wanted to leave. I know it doesn't make sense to you why I did, but I really did have a reason. And I will tell you eventually. When I can figure it all out. But you were right. Hunter died because of me. And I was wasting my abilities. I was. I was afraid too. Of me. Of my abilities. Of losing you. Hurting you. But you're right. I was awful. You can hate me, I would understand."

Jewel stood stunned at my words. As if she was processing her thoughts. She calculated her next move carefully. I could tell because it was written all over her face, just like it always was. Then, she took a big step forward and wrapped me in a massive welcoming hug.

"I don't hate you," she whispered.

I stood stunned for a moment. Unsure of everything. Then, as if I had no control over it, I wrapped my arms around her and hugged my friend back.

thirteen

After a restful night's sleep in my own dorm room, and in my own bed, I found myself waking to welcome the sunrise. There was a peaceful silence about the dorms at such an early hour, one that I had completely forgotten about.

I tiptoed across my room to the pile of snacks and carefully opened the wrapper of a slightly stale snack bar. The sound of my chewing pierced through the serenity of the morning silence inside of my ears. I clicked on the light of my closet and peered inside as I munched on my morning snack.

There were so many pieces of clothing here with so many memories attached, and it felt odd to be looking at them all without the lingering fog that I had lived in for so many months. Picking out an outfit to wear, I flicked the light back off and got myself ready for the day.

My brush remained in the same spot that Jewel left it the last time she brushed through my hair. I found myself filled with odd confidence as I styled myself and prepared my mind for reentering the reality of my life. With a final look in the mirror, I nodded with satisfaction and was completely ready to take the steps to move on from dwelling on the past, and Hunter's absence.

A glimpse of movement caught my eye as the air from the vent toyed with the stack of unopened letters from home. Memories stung in my chest as I thought of Mom, Dad, and Bray. Turning, I took the steps toward the letters with feet that felt like they were made of lead. I took one of the envelopes in my hand, catching a whiff of the slight scent of Mom's blueberry muffins as I broke open the seal.

My mom's handwriting was just as beautiful

and elegant as ever. So much of her personality was shown in the letters of blue ink on the pages. She talked of Dad's trips, and Bray being his silly self. I opened another from her, and she talked about how the ice cream shop had new flavors they experimented with. Some of them were, apparently, not very good.

As I worked my way through the pile of letters, I found myself smiling and thinking of Athra. Thinking of sitting around the table with them enjoying dinner. Having peanut butter late at night in Bray's room. I thought of how my dad's wings lit up when he talked with Mom sometimes. And how Dad would come back energized after delivering goods. I thought of Hunter's parents. I remembered Ruby and our chats over tea.

Ruby and Jan would have gotten along well, I think. Jan's face came to mind, and I smiled for a moment, happy to have crossed paths with her. I owed it to her, just as much as myself, to learn my power and conquer the fear laced inside me. I tossed a coat on and exited the room into the quiet halls. Cautiously, I tapped on Jewel's door. To my surprise, she opened it right away.

"You're actually up?" I whispered with

surprise.

"Well, you said that you wanted to go in early today," she noted.

I nodded with relief. *She remembered.*

She tied up her boot, flicked her head to the side as if to ask "ready?" I nodded and smiled back. Jewel threw an arm around my shoulder, and we headed out of the dorms.

It was like the fight between us had never happened. We didn't miss a beat, and she treated me just the same as she always had. Though it felt odd, I embraced it, happy to have one less thing to worry about, and elated to have her by my side. I was also thankful to have had the evening before to talk and break the ice between us. And just as she promised, nothing changed, and we would go back to being pals.

As we stepped outside into the crisp morning air, a light fog drifted around at our feet against the shoveled path. Jewel glanced between the fog and my face. She began to hop out of pure glee, trying, and failing, to contain her excitement.

"What?" I asked with a chuckle.

"Want to see something?" she asked. She didn't wait for me to answer and half-dove for the fog on the ground. "Okay, okay. So, you know how fog is not, like, its own substance. It's basically tiny droplets of water, right? So, it got me thinking, if I can mold liquid, then I can play with fog, right? I mean it doesn't quite work *exactly* the same, but it's close enough, right?"

Jewel took the fog in her hands. I watched as she molded it and smoothed it. It would escape her grip for a moment, and then she would try again. Molding and smoothing, molding and smoothing, gathering and smoothing, until finally she stood and presented her art. A deformed, starting-to-topple snowman. *Fog-man, I suppose.*

"Ta-da!" she announced, flourishing her hands to present her creation.

"He's falling over," I noted, pretending to be unimpressed.

She flashed me a grumpy look that made her look like a small child and drooped her shoulders. Her fog-man figure escaped from her palms.

"I'm kidding!" I laughed. "That's pretty neat."

She brushed her hands off and looked at me smugly. "Huh!" she huffed. "Top that!"

"Okay," I said nonchalantly.

With one hand still tucked in my pocket, I

crouched and gently reached down toward the fog. I felt each and every molecule, each droplet of moisture and movement. I flicked my fingers and sent out a ripple of tiny, lilac-colored flickers of sparking Energy into the fog. I watched it glitter and jolt as it raced away, eventually fading and becoming consumed by the fog, once again.

Standing once again, I tucked a stray strand of hair behind my ear and glanced at Jewel. Her mouth was open, and she stood dumbfounded. I gave in to the smirk spreading across my pursed lips as I looked her over.

I shrugged smugly. "You told me to top it."

"You—I—when—" she stuttered, attempting to place all her thoughts into a sentence.

I shoved my hands into my pockets and strolled along the path toward the school. "You coming, Jewel?"

I heard a quick giggle as Jewel rushed cautiously to join me, taking care not to slip on the icy ground. A gentle breeze tossed curls of fog mystically around us. Anxious excitement bubbled inside my chest as we rounded the corner, and I could see the academy before us. I enjoyed the feeling of Jewel's happiness beside me while we strolled.

My moment of bliss was suddenly swept away by the sight of a well-put-together brunette standing in our path just outside the academy. Belleza's pink glossed lips curled, and she flashed me a scheming smile. My heart pounded in my chest with the inevitable encounter.

"I heard you were back," Belleza's voice cut through the morning air.

"You're here early," I noted, trying to suppress my agitation.

"Oh, didn't Jewel tell you? Our teacher sees potential in me and is now giving me some private lessons to further my abilities. She wanted me to come in for an early lesson today," Belleza bragged, raising her chin high. *She is so full of herself.*

"Are you sure she doesn't just think you need extra practice because you are behind?" I asked mockingly.

Belleza took in a sharp breath. She gawked with a shrill in her voice. "What do you know? You haven't even been here?"

I shrugged at her, pretending not to care.

"Why are you back? No one wants you here. You are just a danger. You don't belong here. You should have just stayed gone!" Belleza sneered.

Part of me wished at that moment that I did just that. That I hadn't returned. *Was she right? Maybe you don't really belong here, Es. Wait! Am I actually listening and siding with Belleza? Of all people?* I shook my head.

"Maybe you don't belong here, Belleza," I breathed as I glared at her. My anger was getting the best of me.

Her face turned sour, and she let out a heated breath. She lifted a hand, and, for a moment, I could feel a shift in the energy around me. She brought the hand toward me, ever so slightly.

Instinctively, I snatched her wrist. Her eyes widened in surprise, and she shifted in her fancy olive-green, knee-high boots. My thumb lay gently against her soft skin, and I could feel the thumping of her heartbeat grow faster. I felt that shift of energy even more clear. It was her power lingering somewhere inside her. How strong she really could be. What made it tick...

I let go of her hand without a word. She just stared at me, confused and irritated. Jewel didn't say anything, which surprised me.

Belleza lowered her hand and gave a huff with

a roll of her eyes. She turned swiftly, allowing her long brown hair to sway at her back as she disappeared into the academy. I finally turned to look at Jewel and could see her pressing her lips firmly together, suppressing her emotional words inside. She looked as if she were going to burst.

The feeling of her power lingered in my mind for a moment longer. It reminded me of the pressure I felt from everyone around me back in North District. I could feel her need to release her power. It was strange as well as invigorating.

"Why is she so — so — so — Belleza!" Jewel grunted finally, taking me off guard.

I smiled. Seeing her be emotional was almost comforting. Shaking my head at her, I reached for the door.

I sucked a deep breath in as I closed the doors and welcomed the academy's nostalgic aroma to my senses. An echoing sounded in the open space before us, and we were met by Mr. Higgens. He was dressed just as pristine as usual in a navy suit accessorized by a paisley patterned tie and ornately carved cane in hand.

"Good morning, ladies," he greeted with a nod. "Welcome back, Esmari. I take it that your trip did you some good."

"Hello, Mr. Higgens. Yes, I think it did," I greeted.

"Anything new come from your adventure that you want to report?" Mr. Higgens inquired. He seemed intrigued and made it seem like he already knew something but didn't let on to just what he knew.

"Well, I learned some about myself, as well as my powers." Memories danced in my head about the events over the past couple of weeks as I reminisced for a moment. *Where do I begin?*

"I see," Mr. Higgens sighed, waiting for my answer.

"I suppose the most notable is that what we were calling my Energy power seems to have another name as well. Supposedly, I am a Sage. And possibly a—" I hesitated. *Possibly a True Sage? But who knows if that old man was talking any sense? He wasn't all there in the head.*

"Yes?" Mr. Higgens prompted.

I thought for a moment and glanced at Mr. Higgens. "Well, I'm not entirely sure how reliable my information is. But maybe something called a True Sage?"

Mr. Higgens scratched his head for a moment in thought. "I see."

"Wow! Es, that's so cool!" Jewel exclaimed. I had almost forgotten she was there.

"Have you heard of a True Sage before?" I asked quickly.

"Sage, no. A True, yes! They are like long-lost legends. Myths. Fairytales!" Jewel waved her arms around as she spoke. "I mean, they once existed, but suddenly, they just didn't exist anymore. People kind of blamed the mix of Royals and Accompanying Non-Royals for it. You know, mixing bloodlines. But it doesn't make sense anyway. Just sounds ridiculous. And especially being that you are from a Non-Royal bloodline. I mean—"

"Jewel?" I tried to gain her attention back.

She rambled on without noticing. "Which of course you said the information may not be reliable. If that's the case, then the whole theory is blown out of the water. But a True is something spectacular! I guess. Supposed to be, anyway. I mean, I've never met one. Except you, that is, you know, if you are one—"

"Jewel?" I tried again.

"I mean, in that case. If you are a True, that opens a whole world of questions and—" She paused, finally glancing at me. "Oh sorry, did you say something?"

Mr. Higgens gave out a hearty, deep chuckle, leaving Jewel with the look of confusion plastered on her face. I gave her a pat on her arm, and she smiled sheepishly.

"Well, now, a Sage, you say?" Mr. Higgens pondered, adjusting his cane in his hand.

"Yes, I think Sage power and Energy power are one and the same. Just the name changed over time maybe. More so I am a Sage with an Energy power," I shrugged. "Though, it doesn't seem to make any difference to me what it's called. However, I am still figuring out the True part."

"A True is a Mixer. More specifically, a Mixer with two very particular complementing powers. In essence, if you are a Mind Sight, then you would need a complementing power. From what I gather, and from what you seem to have learned, then a Sage, or Energy power, so-to-speak, is a complimenting power. I have heard of Sages, though Banshui hasn't had one since well before my years. Being that we don't have many records of it—I will speak with Agathin and see if she happens to know any more of this Sage power," Mr. Higgens said, adjusting his cane in his hand.

"That would be great!" I exclaimed a bit more enthusiastically than I had intended.

"I think your little adventure did you some good," Mr. Higgens noted again.

He turned and waved his hand as if to bid us farewell. Jewel looked just as giddy as she did when she was rambling just moments ago. I could see the twinkle in her eye as she mulled over the thoughts in her head.

Before long, we parted ways, and I began to trek my way down the winding hallways to the back of the academy. The light got dimmer the closer I came to the Sight classroom. Taking a breath, I entered the large, heavy door and listened to the booming echo against the brick flooring as I closed it behind me.

"Mr. Sean?" I called out into the space.

There were little piles of books laying at the ends of the bookshelves on the ground. Many were books I don't recall ever being in the room before. Some looked fresh and new, while others looked as if they would disintegrate if I breathed on them.

Mr. Sean's added to the library of books, I see. I heard a rustling in the back office.

"Esmari," Mr. Sean's raspy voice beckoned from his office.

I rounded the corner and strode to the office, with its door propped open. *He must have seen me come in with his Sight.* I carefully approached his office, unsure what type of mood he was going to meet me with.

Peering inside, his small office seemed discombobulated. Mr. Sean stood, back turned to me, hunched over a desk with scraps of paper strewn about. Books were propped open all around on the floor, spread out just enough to walk through like a little maze. The wrinkled hem of his signature trench coat swayed as he compared the notes on the table. Cautiously, I tapped on the door frame.

"I know you're there. You don't have to remind me," he said coldly. *Ah, good ol' Mr. Sean.*

"Right," I whispered under my breath.

"Well?" he prompted.

"Well, what?"

"You ran away."

I could feel agitation burning in my throat. "I

came back."

Mr. Sean nodded. Reaching into his pocket, he retrieved a snack bar. His calloused hand tore open the wrapping and shoved a large bite into his mouth. There was something off about him. More than normal. His demeanor was more chaotic, more frantic.

"Have you gotten anywhere with it?" Mr. Sean asked abruptly.

It? My abilities?

Mr. Sean finally turned to look at me. His eyes were red from lack of sleep, and his hair was a mess. He scratched at his scruffy beard. "Your power. Have you progressed any with it?"

I nodded. Lifting my hand, I flicked a lavender puff of Energy and played with it along my fingertips. I listened to its static-like nature in the quiet space for a moment before snuffing it out into my palm.

Mr. Sean's eyes widened ever so slightly. And, if I am not mistaken, I think I saw a glimmer of pride flash across his pupils. "You are able to control it now," he stated.

"Getting there, yes. Supposedly, this power makes me something called a Sage," I explained.

"Sage. A Sage," Mr. Sean mumbled to himself in thought. He whirled around and shuffled through the piles of papers on his desk. He snatched one and held it up to his face glancing over it quickly. "Which would mean—yes—here we go—"

"Mr. Sean?" I asked cautiously.

He whacked the paper with the back of his hand satisfied with the notes scratched all over in blue and black ink. "Yes!"

"Sir?"

"Come with me," Mr. Sean ordered through another mouthful of snack bar as he clumped past me.

fourteen

I followed Mr. Sean out of the office to one of the stacks of books. He was determined and tunnel-visioned. I didn't know what to make of it.

He tossed one book after another to the side, finally settling on a small dirty book. Shoving the last bit of his breakfast in his mouth, he stuffed the wrapper in his trench coat pocket and glanced over the cover of the book. Satisfied, he tucked it under his arm and continued to the podium.

"What does it feel like? When you use the Energy power?" Mr. Sean asked finally.

"Uh—" I thought for a moment. "Electricity. Pressure, I suppose. Burning inside me."

He nodded. "If what you say is true, and you are a Sage with this Energy power. Then you aren't just any Mixer."

"I'm a True Sage."

"How—" Mr. Sean muttered.

"An old man from a book shop said so," I noted.

Mr. Sean's eyes flicked at me as if knowing who I was talking about. His jaw clenched and he furrowed his brow for a moment. I shifted uncomfortably but didn't press him further on the matter.

"There's something I don't understand," I thought aloud. "Well, actually a couple of things. First of all, if you knew, why didn't you tell me?"

"I just did," Mr. Sean croaked.

"Right. Well, why would I be a True Sage and not a True Mind Sight?"

"Don't know."

I sighed. "Why did my Energy power come later?"

"Trauma brought it out. Happens in Mixers sometimes. Don't know for sure, though."

I allowed an irritated huff to escape my mouth. "Well, what *do* you know?"

Mr. Sean took in a large breath, nostrils flaring ever so slightly. Then he swallowed and nodded. "From the only info I can find, there are mentionings of Mixers with Mind Sight and some sort of other power that is connected to everythin'. It is vague in its description and namin'. But one source mentions the name Sage, and another has a couple words about the feeling of electricity. Somewhere else, mentions the pricklin' feelin' of Energy." Mr. Sean pinched his brow for a moment. "So, from what I gather, a Sage and Energy seem to be one and the same. Energy is like a blanket term for the type of power. Like being a Sight. But a Sage is a refined version of someone with Energy power. Someone who can control it, maybe? Being a Mixer with two particular powers makes you a True. Maybe, your dominant ability is the Energy power?"

I remained quiet as I listened to him thinking through it all aloud.

"This is just what I piece together, though.

Could be more to it," Mr. Sean noted, giving another squeeze at his brow.

"I—" I started.

"Enough about that," Mr. Sean interrupted. "How's your Mind Sight? Have you progressed any with that? Or are you still lettin' it control you?"

"Well—" I hesitated. *Anything you say is not going to be the answer he's looking for, Es.*

"Have you practiced anythin' with your little hiatus?" Mr. Sean muttered under his breath.

Frustration filled me. I was agitated. Furious suddenly. I wanted to say so many things to him. I wanted to lash back. Instead, I held my tongue. I let out a heated sigh.

Glaring down the back of Mr. Sean's messy-haired head, I reached down for the floor. I wanted to prove him wrong. More than anything, I wanted to prove to myself that the so-called hiatus was worth it.

Carefully, I placed my fingertips against the cool, dusty, brick flooring. I didn't close my eyes. I kept staring down Mr. Sean. I thought of what I wanted to see; I remembered my encounter with Mr. Higgens this morning. My gut told me something was different about him today. Voluntarily, I released a surge of power from my fingerprints.

My surroundings fell away, and I was whisked into a Sight episode. There were students. Not many. A clock ticked on the wall. I could hear a woman's voice. The instructor of the classroom. She was welcoming Mr. Higgens to the room. He seemed to be looking for something. Scanning the room discreetly. He smiled, pretending as if he did not have an alternative motive.

I stayed on him. He waved the teacher on, inviting her to continue her instructions. After another scan through the room, I could see him analyzing, observing. With a nod to the teacher, he exited the room, and I drifted away from the Sight episode.

Mr. Sean was leaning against the wall, scanning through the book he had retrieved. Carefully, I stood and shook out my sleepy legs. I took a sigh and watched as Mr. Sean's scowl flicked toward me.

"What is going on with Mr. Higgens?" I asked flatly.

Mr. Sean's eyes narrowed as he carefully

considered my words. He offered me no response. I clenched my teeth. *Does he know?*

"You are still controlled by your Sight," he scoffed as he looked back at the book.

Glancing around, I could feel my heart pounding inside of my chest as resentment burned in my throat. *Fine. I will prove to you I can control it. You don't believe me? Then I will prove it!* I looked at the book in his rough hands and could feel a sly vengeance beam inside me. *Just what are you reading, Mr. Sean?*

I pressed a fingertip against the floor again. I felt his presence before me. How he held the book. How he stood, leaned against the wall. I released a small surge again and launched another Mind Sight episode. The book came to me as if I were reading it myself. The page read "Control and connection of Sight and power." Pulling myself away from the episode, I allowed my lips to curl into a smirk. I stood sure and eager to prove myself to him.

"Control and connection of Sight and power," I recalled back to him. "Is this a lesson for me or you?"

I watched as the realization washed over his

face. His eyes filled with irritation and surprise over my pride. Quickly, he snapped the book shut and returned the scowl to his brow. His mouth twitched as he had an internal argument with himself.

Finally, after what felt like ages of being suppressed by his glaring scowl, he glanced back at his book and sat against the wall. He waved a hand to me as if to ask me to join him in sitting.

"Tell me, what do you feel when you are in a Sight episode?" Mr. Sean asked.

I shrugged. "Depends."

"What about when you are around anyone else? Have you had contact with anyone using their power? Physically touching them?" Mr. Sean continued.

A flash of memory to this morning with Belleza ran through my mind. I clenched my jaw, thinking of the power running through her veins. I didn't want to answer him. Something about it made me uncomfortable.

He grunted to himself, almost as if he was unsatisfied with his own question. "No. Never mind that." He closed his eyes. "What happens in one of your Mind Sight episodes. How do you feel?

How do you gravitate towards something?"

I shrugged again. "I'm drawn to something, I guess."

Mr. Sean nodded, and if I wasn't mistaken, I think he was actually satisfied with the answer I gave. "Okay, good start. Try gravitatin' to me in your Sight episode again."

"Now?" I asked.

"Yes, now. When else would I be talkin' about?" Mr. Sean sassed.

"What am I looking for?" I asked. His instructions were so vague I felt confused and lost.

He closed his eyes for a moment and shoved his hand in his pocket. He brought out a small scrap of paper with something scribbled on it. "Read this."

It felt odd to be working on a lesson with him, for once, rather than straight from a book this time. He seemed so different, so much more frazzled and unconventional since before. Though, I wasn't necessarily objecting to some legitimate instruction time.

I swallowed hard and pressed a fingertip against the grooved brick. I thought about the paper in his calloused, tired hand. Releasing a surge of energy from the pad of my index finger, I immediately saw the paper. The scrap of paper had plenty of scribbles on it, all barely legible, and lots of the words scribbled out.

From what I could make out of it, there were page numbers all over, with a few words here or there. In the center, the words "Volume one." For a moment, I felt an odd sensation about it. The scribbles had a presence about them, like an imprint of someone else. Not Mr. Sean.

I pulled away from the episode and back to where I sat. Retracting my fingers from the floor, I folded my hands in my lap and thought about the mess of words on the scrap of paper. *What was the point of that? I already knew I could see something in your hand. You knew that.*

"Well?" Mr. Sean prompted.

"It's a load of scribbles and something about Volume one of a book maybe?" I noted.

"Yes. Okay good."

The ticking from the clock on the wall echoed in the room, counting our moments of silence during the pause in our conversation. I glanced at Mr. Sean's boots, searching for something to occupy my brain as I waited for him to say something more.

The toes were scuffed up, and one shoelace dangled half untied, as if it had given up on the conversation as well. The moment was so strained, and I couldn't take the silence any longer.

"So, what was that about? You already knew I could do that?" I finally inquired.

"Look at it again," Mr. Sean said, his head still tilted back with his eyes shut, as he leaned against the wall behind him.

"Why?" I asked, feeling like the lesson was repetitive and pointless. *I almost wish you just gave me a book to work on again.*

"Look at it again. Tell me more."

"Why do you have it if it's not yours anyway?" I asked.

His eyes flew open, and he studied me. *What did I say wrong now?* I looked him over, too, trying to read his expression. There was fear inside his eyes. It was reserved, confused, and most of all, intrigued.

"How?" he asked. It was such a plain and simple word with such a complex indication.

"The writing, it felt different from your presence," I noted. *Good job, Es. You sound as crazy as he is.*

Mr. Sean looked at the paper. He studied it. I could see him thinking. Analyzing. Planning. He was suspended in time, floating along with the ticks of the wall clock. Processing whatever was going on in his mind.

I didn't move. I didn't dare to breathe. And just when I was beginning to think he forgot I was there, he looked up. He looked at me with his icy blue eyes once so full of sorrow, and for the first time since I had met him, he allowed the corner of his lips to curl into a smile filled with hope.

fifteen

Mr. Sean became eager to teach me following that day. It was odd at first, but I think both he and I grew to enjoy the lessons. It was as if I was finally beginning to understand my power. My Mind Sight, at least.

I don't know exactly what it was that I said for him to change his way of teaching, but I was grateful for the opportunity. Though, I wouldn't go as far as to say he was nice or anything to me. He was still his bitter self most days, but something about that was surprisingly comforting, in a weird way.

I found the lessons he was gravitating toward were all on the obscure side of things, but it was nice to be challenged. He would focus on one trick, so-to-speak, one day, and then the next, something completely different. But I couldn't help but feel that it was all connected, and I found myself trusting him and his teachings more as the weeks went on.

"So, you say he's actually teaching you. Like a normal, I don't know, teacher?" Jewel teased as we exited our dorm building.

It had been weeks since we both had a day free of classes. Our schedules seemed to rarely match up since Mr. Sean increased his lessons, and Jewel began to train with her instructor outside of her regular lessons. I rolled my eyes at her comment and gave her a gentle shove.

"I'm serious. I'm not just reading through random books anymore. He's guiding me and teaching me how to do all sorts of things," I defended. "Like the other day, I was learning how to understand the presence of a Royal versus a

Non-Royal in my Mind Sight episode."

"That's neat. Odd. But, neat," Jewel noted.

"What do you mean it's odd?" I asked.

"Well, why is that important?" Jewel mentioned.

"I—" I thought about it for a moment. "Well, I don't exactly know why that might be important. At least, not yet. And I'm not very good at it, currently. But I'm sure it has to do with something I will learn later."

"Probably," Jewel agreed. "Hey, have you thought anything about what will happen after the academy?"

The question was abrupt and caught me off guard. "What do you mean?"

"Like, when you're all done with lessons here, and is time for you to make a choice on what you want to do next?" Jewel said.

"No, I really hadn't gotten that far. I've only been here for a little while anyway. Why? Have you?" I asked.

"No. It's just something my teacher asked me recently and it got me thinking," she noted.

Jewel shrugged. Though my curiosity was getting the best of me, I silenced it and decided to drop the topic. I listened to the sound of the soles of our shoes sloshing in the muddy sludge below us. We hadn't had fresh snowfall in days, and what we were left with was mounds of brown ice, piled up to the sides of the pathways.

"Maybe we should just fly there?" Jewel suggested.

I nodded in agreement as I caught myself from slipping on yet another hidden patch of ice. I stabilized myself cautiously, and I could feel Jewel's eyes on me. Quickly, I glanced up to see a giddy look spreading across her face.

"What?" I asked, finding myself afraid of the answer to come.

She flicked her eyebrows at me slyly and fluttered into the sky with her cellophane iridescent wings glinting in the late morning sun. "Race you to the Dripping Crown!" she called over her shoulder.

"You got a head start, that's no fair!" I jokingly wined.

"It's only a fair race if I *do* get a head start!" she shouted back.

I shook my head and flicked out my wings behind me. The crisp air felt nice on my wingtips. I flicked a puff of Energy to my nail and enjoyed the sensation as my wings filled out to the fullest.

Darting up into the sky, I caught glimpses of color reflecting off iced-over objects all around me. It was like I was leaving a glittering trail behind me as I flew. I could see my friend in the near distance ahead of me, her copper smear glinting each time she flapped.

Quickly, I cut through the air, weaving this way and that to avoid trees as I sailed up into the sky over Banshui. The air was still, and the world seemed quiet as if it were waiting patiently for something to happen. And for a moment, something felt off. Like the air of Banshui knew something I didn't.

Shaking the feeling from my shoulders, I came up to Jewel and felt a smirk spread across my face. She was so determined and focused, and I knew I was about to crush her hopes of winning.

"Hi, Jewel!" I greeted.

I darted around her and felt the wind from her wings press against the corners of mine. I could feel her falter slightly and then force herself to go a little faster. It was no use. A couple of extra flicks of my wings, and I passed her with ease.

"Bye, Jewel!" I called back to her.

I felt her falling away slightly just as The Dripping Crown came into view. The air grew warmer as we crossed into Coastal District. The shoreline in the distance was an enchanting sight this time of year. I landed shortly on the porch just outside the door of the business as it sat suspended up in the air, and I chuckled at the squeaking sound of the sign swinging overhead in the salty breeze just beginning for the day. Before long, Jewel landed beside me in a huff.

"Why— do I—do this— to myself?" she panted.

I chuckled and gave her a look of pity, just as we heard a loud crash from inside the door. We flicked looks of concern to each other and scrambled for the door. The jingle for the bell over the door echoed in the fairly empty establishment.

A loud drawn-out sigh came from the man behind the counter. He turned around, and we watched as foam dripped from his chin. An equally messy hand retrieved the wire-rimmed glasses from his face and gave them a quick shake, flinging drips of drink around him. Smearing white foam from his chin, he revealed his unmistakable orange goatee. *Oh, Victor.*

Jewel let out a hearty laugh, and Victor caught sight of the both of us standing in the doorway. His shoulders fell, realizing how foolish he probably looked. I couldn't help but giggle, too.

"You look like the snow monster from those children's books we used to read," Jewel giggled, trying to catch her breath.

"Oh, well thank you for making me feel *so* good about myself, Jewels," Victor commented sarcastically as he rolled his eyes at her. "You know what? Just for that, you can make your own drinks!"

"Hey! We are paying customers here, mister," Jewel pouted playfully as we approached the counter.

"Okay, okay," Victor laughed. "Could you at least toss me that towel there?"

Jewel snatched the damp white towel from the edge of the counter and tossed it toward Victor, who caught it with ease, even without his glasses on his face. Victor smeared the foam from his skin and whipped his glasses clean before returning them to their rightful place at the bridge of his nose.

"Alright, what are you ladies having?" Victor asked, taking the flat cap from his head, and wiping the speckles of foam from its brim.

I nodded to Jewel to order first. I watched as she rocked back and forth, debating what flavor she needed for a day like today. After she finally made her decision and I had made mine, we headed up to the loft as we waited for our beverages. It was odd being here without Hunter, but while his missing presence still stung a little, it was also nice to be in a familiar space once more.

Jewel babbled on about how she wished the weather would warm up. Her excitement over the seasons changing was something I simply didn't understand. She talked all about how the weather smelled different when spring was on its way in Banshui. Trying her best, she described the "feeling in the breeze" being the indicator that warmth and spring days were on the horizon. But apparently, it was just something I would have to wait and experience for myself.

"Order up!" Victor announced, bringing the drinks up the stairs. "Vanilla cinnamon blend for Jewel, and a hot capp' for Es."

"Thanks," I nodded as I retrieved the mug

from Victor's outstretched arm and placed it on the table before me. I stuck my hands in my lap and leaned against the wooden railing as I watched the steam rise up from the cup.

"Hey, uh, Es," Victor stuttered. He sat down and grabbed his flat cap from his head uncomfortably.

"Yeah?" I prompted, knowing exactly where this was going.

"Es, I'm—uh—I'm sorry, you know, about Hunter," Victor mumbled, ringing the cap in his soft, unsure hands.

"Yeah, thanks. Me, too," I responded, my voice laced with so much understanding, it even surprised my own ears.

"It's really good to see you in here," Victor noted and glanced at Jewel. Suddenly, a smirk crossed his lips. "Maybe I won't have to listen to Jewel go on and on about how worried she is about you anymore. She just wouldn't stop rambling about it day in, and day out—"

"Hey!" Jewel scoffed and gave him a quick shove. "I don't ramble!"

Victor and I glanced at each other. "Yeah, you do," we teased in unison.

Jewel opened her mouth once more to protest, but promptly let out a sigh and took a slurp of her drink instead with defeat. I chuckled under my breath as I also reached for my mug. Blowing at the steamy liquid, I took a sip and allowed for the warmth to seep down my throat. The bell over the door jingled, and Victor excused himself to help his new customer.

I found myself distracted and partially unable to focus on Jewel's story she was explaining with great enthusiasm. Every so often, I would half-tune back in and catch a few words of her voice, then feel myself lost in foggy thought. My mind wandered more than normal. Though the same feeling as I had earlier in the day danced across my skin. Something was off, but I couldn't quite figure out what.

"Es? Hello?" Jewel was waving her hand in front of my face to gather my attention. "You zoned out again."

"Sorry," I quickly apologized, running my hand through my hair.

"You think a Sight episode would help?" Jewel offered.

I shrugged. I felt as if I were being pulled in

two directions. Not really here, and not really needing to use my power. Somewhere in the middle, I suppose. I took a sigh. *Maybe your Sight needs you to see something, Es.*

"Go ahead, I'll go help Victor for a few and give you some space," Jewel urged with a smile. She stood, snagging her cup and heading for the stairs.

Okay. I tried to stifle the uneasy feeling inside my chest and adjusted my sitting position on the floor. Something was telling me that I would be here a while. I pressed my palm to the floor in front of me and allowed my power to seep from it in a relaxed release.

A scene appeared before me, so clear that I felt as if I were there. It was calm. A few people were somewhere near. Unfamiliar.

Before me was some sort of grand tent. I wanted to enter. I willed myself to enter. Somehow, it worked. Something about the space reminded me of an episode in the past. This wasn't inside of Banshui. I listened. Waiting to know why I was there. Why I needed to be there. What I needed to see.

Someone entered the tent behind me. Their

presence wafted by where I was, completely unaware. An individual crept from the shadow, his black feathered wings a telling sign of his identity. I was in Byrein's tent.

"Report," Byrein's voice sneered at his guest.

"She's back. We found her. She's under the watch of the academy. Of your father." The Ex spoke to Byrein with a tone of worry. She turned to reveal a soft face. Her thin, light blonde hair danced in the light.

"How did she look?" Byrein asked, tilting his head dreamily.

"She, well," the Ex paused. "The girl looked strong. She looks like she's becoming a great successor for you."

I watched as Byrein nodded. His obsession was more evident in his cold dark eyes today. The woman left his tent without another word.

"Ah, Esmari," Byrein whispered to himself. He bit his lip, his gaze fell directly on where I was, still completely unaware of my presence. "You grow so strong. Imagine what you could do with my guidance. Imagine what we could do together. You and me. Side by side. Yes, I will have you as my own. I will make you so happy."

I pulled myself from the Sight episode. My heart pounded inside my chest so loudly that it made the blender downstairs a muffled hum. The way Byrein talked of me, it was apparent.

He didn't just want to teach me. He wanted more. *Just what does he want from me?* I shuddered at the thought. His obsession I felt for me was evident. I knew the answer.

I think he wants me to be his wife.

sixteen

"No, no," I shook my head at myself. "No, Es. You could be wrong. You have to be wrong." I shifted uncomfortably and reached for my now-cold cappuccino. I took a long, drawn-out sip to calm my nerves just as Jewel came back up the stairs to the loft to rejoin me.

"You were there a while. Feel any better?" Jewel asked chipperly.

I reached for my necklace. *Only you saw that,*

Es. She doesn't have to know. "Yeah, much better." I lied through a smile.

"Anything to report?" Jewel asked. I winced at the word report, remembering Byrein's use of the very same word.

"No," I said, offering my friend no additional information. I could feel her quizzical gaze fall on me, but she left it alone.

The bell over the door chimed once more, and I could suddenly feel the presence of some Non-Royal individuals. A familiar voice drifted up to the loft where Jewel and I relaxed. Jewel's face lit up with recognition. She popped up to her feet and looked over the railing to the people just below.

"Hi, guys!" Jewel greeted. She flicked a look at me. "I invited Finn and the guys to hang out today, hope you don't mind."

The surprised look on my face must have scared her.

"You don't mind, right, Es? I mean, if that wasn't okay, I can just tell them we will arrange a different day—" Jewel babbled.

"No, no. I'm glad you invited them." I smiled. *Anything to take my mind off of Byrein.*

Moz and Darren clumped up the stairs and

fought to see who would greet us fastest. I laughed at their competitive nature. The two smiled at us with big grins.

"Hi, guys," I chuckled.

"Hey, so we were thinking maybe we could all head over to the beach for the afternoon. What do you say?" Moz invited with excitement.

"Oh, that sounds like fun!" Jewel said.

"Cool!" Darren chimed, his wings flicking on his back. He leaned over the glossy wooden railing and called down, "Hey, Finn, make them to-go. We are going to the beach!"

After the boys gathered their drinks from Victor, we collected our things to head out. I brought our dirty mugs to the counter for Victor and thanked him.

"No problem," Victor nodded. "Hey, Es. Don't be a stranger."

I smiled back at him, before taking my leave and joining everyone outside. Together we flew toward the beach.

Something in me clicked. Like what I had been practicing with Mr. Sean suddenly made sense. The feeling of powered individuals and non-powered. Royals and Non-Royals. I could feel their essence beside me in the air as they flew. I could almost *see* the power on Jewel's skin, on her wings. And, just for a moment, I knew that if I wanted to, I could touch it, too.

We landed on the soft beach sand soon after. A cold breeze covered in ocean salt kissed our cheeks in a lovely welcome. The beach was barren, making it feel like we owned the whole place.

Jewel linked arms with me, and we strolled along the soft sand, attempting not to pull each other down as we ventured. Finn and Darren were running after Moz, chasing him down and teasing him for something he said that I didn't quite catch. Jewel and I giggled at their childishness.

I watched our feet as we walked, enjoying how each grain of sand shifted away from our shoes. The coarse substance beneath our feet, so firm, yet so much vulnerability from outside pressure. I focused on this, rather than the feeling of Jewel's arm on mine. Her power sitting on her skin like a layer of lotion never soaking completely in.

"Hey, Es?" Jewel's comforting voice beckoned.

"Huh?" I said, still watching the sand below. *I wonder if I could use the motion and energy in the sand to —*

"Isn't that your teacher?" Jewel asked.

"What? Where?" I responded suddenly. My eyes followed her outstretched arm pointing at a figure in the distance.

"I think, you're right," I said. "I've never seen him outside of the classroom."

"Me either!" Jewel noted.

I chuckled for a moment. "I honestly thought he lived there!"

Jewel gave out a big bout of laughter as we both thought of that possibility. "Do you think he used the books as his pillow?"

"Well, he's always there before I come, and always there long after I leave!" I giggled. "And I'm pretty sure he survives off of snack bars for all of his meals!"

Mr. Sean was standing near the ocean staring out as if he was trying to understand all the complexities of life. Though he was deep in thought, he looked less troubled than he normally did. However, I was certain that just the environment was making it seem that way.

"I suppose I should acknowledge him," I sighed.

Jewel nodded and released my arm so I could

continue on my own toward my teacher. The closer I came, the less I knew what to expect out of him.

"Esmari," Mr. Sean greeted flatly.

"Hello, Mr. Sean," I said in return. It was odd and uncomfortable. I searched for something more to say. "I'm surprised to see you out here. Didn't think you liked public places much."

"It's not very *public* today," he noted, referring to the lack of people.

"True," I agreed.

Another breeze brushed by us and toyed with our silence. I tucked a hand in my pocket and listened to the waves against the sand. Glancing up at Mr. Sean's face, I saw his eyes slowly close. His presence, his energy, surrounding his figure was apparent to me. I could feel the presence of his power lessen the moment his eye flickered shut.

"You see it, don't you?" Mr. Sean said, calmly opening his eyes again.

"I—"

"It was the same for Byrein. It was obvious the day that his Mind Sight allowed him to see the power of a Royal." Mr. Sean spoke in such a relaxed way that I wasn't sure what to make of it.

I nodded. Glancing over at Moz and Darren as

they took part in a foot race, I allowed a smirk to flow across my lips. Moz was falling behind. Darren finished by tagging Finn's hand just as Moz fell face-first into the sand.

"Best two out of three!" Moz called, pulling himself up and dusting off. "And loser has to jump in the icy cold water!"

Darren's smile could be seen from a mile away. "You're on!"

Oh, Moz. You still haven't learned. I shook my head and turned back to Mr. Sean. I saw once again his power strong, gravitating around his eyes, like a mirage on a hot day. I blinked, and it was gone.

"What's it like?" Mr. Sean asked. "Seein' my power?"

"I see where it radiates from, I suppose. For you and Jewel, it's always there. Present. Never dissipated. Sometimes strong, sometimes weak. I see it almost like a barely visible wave one moment, and just feel its presence the next. It feels like its own being," I said. The words seemed to fall from my mouth.

"Like you can touch it?" Mr. Sean asked.

"Yeah, I think so. In a way. Is this why Byrein is interested in me?"

"Have you tried, yet?" Mr. Sean asked, ignoring my question.

"No," I stated, shaking my head.

Mr. Sean remained silent for a moment. He peered thoughtfully at the waves glistening in the sun. "Many Royals of different powers can sense the presence of another powered individual. Mind Sights, however, can actually see the power. They are the only power who can touch someone else's ability," Mr. Sean spoke softly.

"Why is that? Why don't I need to be in a Mind Sight episode to see it?" I pondered.

"Your power gives you the ability to see what others can't. In more ways than one. This is one of those ways," he explained in such a gentle way, it made me wonder if this is how he taught his son.

I nodded for a moment, soaking in his words. I wanted it all to slow down. I felt like every time I figured out my power, my abilities, they evolved. I was constantly changing. My power was constantly changing. Part of me wanted to stop and catch my breath. Part of me enjoyed how quickly it all changed. How quickly I felt like I was learning my own power.

"Go ahead," Mr. Sean said, flicking a glance at

his arm.

"What?" I asked abruptly.

"See what it feels like to touch another's power," Mr. Sean prompted again.

Baffled, I reached a hesitant hand up. *This is crazy. Was he serious?* I looked over his sure and calm face once more. *Here goes.*

By instinct, I took two fingers and pressed them lightly just below Mr. Sean's shoulder. I focused on where his power radiated from, how it moved. A release of power, the same way I released a jolt to enter a Mind Sight episode, happened. I didn't intend to. But my Sight did it for me, without my consent. I was suddenly connected to Mr. Sean's Distance Sight power.

It was an odd, empowering sensation. I knew, if I wanted to, I could manipulate it. I felt how it worked. How it was connected to Mr. Sean. How his power flowed through him all the way to the deformed strands of his wings.

Like a leech draining his everyday energy, I could tell what he could and couldn't do with it. I knew where it was and where it wasn't. I could feel the pain it caused him. I knew if I wanted to, I could just pause it, just for a moment, just long enough to give him relief.

And just for a moment, I did.

His power paused at a pinch of my own power. I felt the relief in tension wash over Mr. Sean like a fresh drink of water on parched lips. I felt his power slowly seep into my fingertips. It was like a slow burn pressing into the pads of my fingers.

No, Es. This isn't right. A small voice inside me beckoned. Quickly, I pushed his power away from me. Away from my fingers. Back to where it came from. And unfortunately, returned Mr. Sean to the discomfort he experienced on the daily.

I pulled my hand away desperately. I didn't know what to make of it. It was invigorating and terrifying. *I had his power, literally, in my hands.* My veins felt empty as if they were already craving for another taste of his power. As if I had deprived them of a sweet treat.

Mr. Sean peered at me, studying me. He didn't say anything for the longest time. I could see him thinking behind his stern eyes. He was considering his next words carefully.

Somewhere in his eyes, I could see a glimmer of hope rising within him. As if I was the answer to his problems. His solution to whatever he was pondering at all times of the day. His wings flicked on his back as if anxiety ridden.

"What took Byrein years to grasp, you figured out in mere seconds," Mr. Sean breathed with a tinge of astonishment behind his coarse voice.

I watched again as Mr. Sean studied me. An obsession clouded his pupils for no longer than a second before he blinked it away. His expression turned from hopeful to conflict. He flashed a look around the beach.

"Hey, Es!" called Finn, waving for me.

"I think I should head back to my friends," I offered, desperate to escape the moment of uncertainty.

Mr. Sean gave a nod and turned back toward the waves. His hands sat in his pockets comfortably, and I felt him close his eyes to relieve his own tension.

I jogged back over to the others. Their excitement was unfazed by my absence. Jewel sat on the sand with her shoes beside her. A salty breeze tossed her hair from side to side as she pulled her jacket tighter around her. She flashed me a warm smile and patted the sand to her side, inviting me to join her.

"What did I miss?" I asked, nodding at Darren, who had Moz in a headlock.

"Well, Moz challenged Darren to a race and lost. But he is refusing to own up to losing. He's supposed to jump into the water. However, he is claiming Darren cheated," Jewel explained, resting her arms on her knees.

"Ah, I see," I sighed.

"Will someone please tell him that he lost?" Darren called out.

"I call for a rematch!" Moz pleaded, breaking free.

"You could always race Es!" Finn called back as he flopped into the sand next to Jewel.

"Why am I always brought into these things?" I chuckled.

"Because we know we will win that bet," Finn smirked.

I nodded and flicked a sly look toward Jewel. I stood up and peered down the way to Moz, who now looked pale in the face. "Well? Let's go! Wing race. Loser not only has to jump in the water but also buys dinner!"

"Oh! You are on!" Moz said. "I have gotten so much faster. I've been practicing lately! You are going down!"

"My money's on Es!" chimed Darren.

"Same," agreed Finn.

"Yeah. No doubt about it. Es will win," Jewel nodded.

"You all have no faith in me," Moz scoffed.

"Still time to back out," I teased.

"No, way. I will prove I am faster. First one to the rocks and back wins!" Moz backfired, jabbing a finger toward his marker.

I nodded, agreeing to his terms, looking out at the bolder protruding from the ocean.

"Alright! Three, two, one, go!" shouted Moz as he took off into the sky.

I waited for a moment. Just long enough to see him take off. With a smirk and adrenaline coursing through my veins, and through my wings, I flicked my finger to summon a purple spark. Purple felt powerful. I felt as my wings filled out behind me and darted up into the air.

Moz flicked a look back at me as if to mock his lead. Realization washed over his face as he saw me effortlessly approach his position. The flickers of color from my wings reflected off the water below. Another few flaps of my wings and I whizzed past him.

"See you at the finish!" I called back.

The cool air filled my lungs, and the mist from a crashing wave cooled my wingtips. I didn't have to, but I flew as fast as my wings would take me, rounding the nearby boulder and our halfway mark. I passed by Moz once more as I approached the finishing line, and he approached the halfway point.

"I sure am hungry!" I mocked, zooming past.

I heard a growl of frustration leave his lips. My wings cut through the air. I felt free. Like just for a moment, it was just my wings and me in the open sky.

I watched my reflection disappear into the white foam as a playful wave collided with the sandy beach. I allowed the sound of the water to flow in my ears, drowning out the rest of the sounds, just one moment more.

The sand met my feet like a soft cloud. I allowed my wings to return to their black form, snuffing out the spark on my fingertip simultaneously. Slowly, I welcomed the sounds of the world back into my ears.

Darren and Finn cheered, and Jewel was shouting and waving her hands above her head. Finn turned toward Jewel and snatched her in a big hug. Quickly realizing what he had done, he released her and turned away shyly, smoothing down his shirt. Jewel giggled nervously, and Darren's eyes widened at what he had just witnessed before him.

A thud sounded beside me followed by loud, labored breathing. I eyed Moz as he tried to catch his breath.

"How—I—I got—so much faster!" he panted.

"So have I," I shrugged.

He groaned and wiped the beads of sweat from his forehead. Slowly, he turned to the waves, realizing there was no backing out. Moz began walking toward the water, defeated.

"Where should we make him take us?" Finn laughed.

"Somewhere good. Maybe that café?" Darren suggested.

Jewel gawked. "Oh, you mean the one with that turkey melt, over in Central District?"

A shift in the breeze caught me off guard. Something was different. Something was off. I glanced toward Mr. Sean, still standing in the same spot as before, and his eyes darted to me. *He noticed, too.* We weren't alone.

"Yeah, yeah, that one! With all the fancy lighting—" Darren continued.

"Stop," I said.

"What, do you have another idea, Es?" Finn asked with a wide grin spread across his face.

"No, really, stop." I tried again. The uneasiness was growing in the air around me.

"What is it?" Jewel asked, starting to catch on. My eyes darted around the emptiness of the beach, frantically searching for the unwelcomed company. The guys continued to banter with one another, talking about how delicious different dishes sounded.

"I said stop!" I demanded abruptly.

Finn and Darren stepped back in surprise. I spun around as I searched the area once more. In the near distance, I could see Moz talking himself up to jump into the icy waters before him.

Sharp pain in my temple sent me crashing to the ground.

"Ah, Esmari. Even more beautiful when you fly!" sneered Byrein's voice inside my head.

My hand squeezed at my skull as if it would help. His voice left a ringing in my ears.

"But the stakes of the race were not interesting

enough. Shouldn't they be more interesting? Just jumping into the water isn't enough after losing to you, my darling."

The excruciating pain ceased, and I was left in a daze. I could feel my blood draining from my face trying to make sense of it all. *Interesting? How was he going to make it more interesting?* I grasped to find my bearings.

Then I felt it. Not one, but two other powered individuals were somewhere nearby. Glancing around, I could see Finn and Jewel next to me now, they were saying something, but I couldn't tell what. Mr. Sean was coming now too.

The sharp pain arose once more.

"You have grown so much. Your power is getting so strong. Let's see just how you handle this."

I caught my breath. *No. You are going to stop this.* I laced my fingers with the loose beach sand below me and pressed a jolt of power from my palms. *Where are you!*

Byrein came to view. Standing next to him was a woman with stringy, long hair. She had an act of vengeance in her eyes.

"When you are ready, Nim. We need to avenge

my Esmari," Byrein instructed. There was a flicker of enjoyment spreading across his lips.

Quickly, I followed her gaze as she looked out at the ocean. Out at Moz just entering the water.

I pulled myself away from the Sight episode, yanking my hands from the sand as I felt a release of pressure, knowing it came from the woman he called Nim. I felt a subtle rumble below the land, unsure of what to make of it.

I gathered my thoughts and spun around, searching for Moz, just as a screech erupted from his lips.

eighteen

A tangle of a seaweed-like root burst from the surface of the water and splashed back down as if it were a creature thrashing in the waves. Without another thought, I sent out a sparking ball of Energy right at it and watched as it withered away into the water. A shock from the impact revealed the path from which it came. The path to the woman called Nim.

Finn and Darren rushed to the water to

retrieve Moz. I had one thing on my mind. To follow that direct path. But Mr. Sean's voice pulled me back.

"Esmari!" he demanded. It stopped me in my tracks. He didn't prompt further. He didn't have to.

What if they are still there? Watching. Suddenly their presence wasn't evident anymore. It was as if they were wafted away with the breeze.

"They're gone, Esmari," Mr. Sean cooed. I knew he was right, but I still found myself glancing at where they once stood.

We watched as Finn and Darren stood Moz up and slung his arms over their shoulders. They inched their way up away from the water, his pantleg stained with red.

"It got me! Whatever that was, it got me!" Moz cried out as they lowered him onto the sand.

Mr. Sean looked at us and furrowed his brow. He scratched at his scruffy chin and flung the length of his trench coat behind him, out of his way. I could see him taking a quick mental note of his next steps.

"Okay, you two. Get out of here!" Mr. Sean barked at Finn and Darren.

"No, we can help. Let us help!" Finn snapped.

Mr. Sean eyed me for a moment. "Finn is learning medicine. He can help," I affirmed.

Mr. Sean pinched the bridge of his nose and let out a grunt. "Fine. You girl. Water girl. Come here."

"Jewel—" she tried, her eyes wide with shock.

"Yeah, whatever. You manipulate liquid, right? Get some of the saltwater off his leg near this gash," Mr. Sean instructed.

"You, Finn, make sure he doesn't pass out or anythin'," Mr. Sean instructed. He turned to me. "Come here, Es. Do everything that I say. Exactly as I say it. Got it?"

I nodded and sat next to Jewel, who was clenching her jaw at the sight of Moz's leg. Darren sat up by his head.

"My leg is burning," Moz groaned.

"You are such a wuss. It's just a scratch," Darren teased, trying to lighten the mood.

Mr. Sean crouched next to me, and it was then that I knew he was going to ask me to do something I wouldn't like.

"Esmari, remember how it felt when you touched my power earlier?" he asked in a hushed tone. I didn't like where this was going. "I need you to do that for your friend here. She has the ability to manipulate liquid. Your friend doesn't know it, but she can also manipulate blood. I need you to help her do so."

I clenched my jaw. *Was he wanting me to manipulate her power? What if I hurt her?*

"Remember, exactly as I say," Mr. Sean urged once more.

"His leg doesn't look right," Finn noted. "I think that was a poisonous root."

Mr. Sean nodded in agreement. "Jewel, Moz has poison in him. I need you to do somethin' for me. I need you to make sure it doesn't spread. Esmari is goin' to help you. What I need you to do is focus on anything else. Just keep your hands right where they are."

Tears welled up in her eyes. "This isn't like water. I don't know what you are asking of me!" Jewel shrieked.

"Jewel. Look at me. Right here," Finn said calmly. "Jewel, just focus on me."

She nodded just as a trembling tear rolled down her cheek.

"Okay, Esmari. Just like before," whispered Mr. Sean. "Reach out for her power."

I took a wavering breath. I wanted to protest. I needed to protest. But, I knew there wasn't time for that. Closing my eyes, I pressed two fingers onto her shoulder blade. I allowed a surge of power to leave me. I felt for her power. How it engulfed her every inch of skin.

"Good now, find the core. Where it resonates from," Mr. Sean whispered.

Out of instinct, I felt my power drift toward hers and connect. I felt how it breathed. How it moved. I felt where it was at all times. I felt how much potential she had…

"Once you have found it. Connect and allow it to show you the way."

I nodded. Then something I couldn't quite explain happened. A sensation stemming from her fingertips to mine on her shoulder blade. It resonated. Reverberated. Throughout her veins. At my power's urging, I released another surge.

"Good, Esmari," Mr. Sean's voice was calm and distant. "Jewel, find the poison."

I felt like I was floating into an empty space. Everything else seemed to be slipping further and further away. I felt the connections of her power with mine. I felt the ability she had. How much more she could be. I felt as her power shifted at my fingertips. It curled with a twitch of my skin.

I wanted to see what she could do. I wanted to understand it. To push it to its limits. I wanted to make it more than what it was. I wanted to make this change to her power permanent.

"Ah, Esmari, my dear." Byrein's voice echoed in the emptiness. "Your ability is intoxicating. You are so much more powerful than I thought. You are so much stronger than I imagined. You will make a great leader to our kind. Alongside me, as my woman. We can be the perfect pair. Imagine what we will accomplish together."

I felt as though someone was ripping me out of the sky. Falling through the emptiness. Falling back down to the solid ground. I knew the sensation would stop, but I didn't want it to. I could feel Jewel's power at the mercy of my hand. It was mine to alter at whim.

No, Esmari, you have to stop. Esmari, stop. Esmari! Don't do this. You aren't like him. You are better than this. You know where to draw the line. Don't do this! Esmari! Stop!

"Esmari! It's finished!" Mr. Sean's desperate voice came crashing into my ears.

I pulled away from Jewel's power, detaching from its potential and returning it to the state I encountered it. It was like a shockwave echoing through every fiber of my being.

Yanking my hand away from her shoulder blade, I could feel as tears welled up inside me. Tears of terror. Tears of utter confusion. I reached for the charms on my necklace and rubbed the stones against the pads of my fingers.

"Esmari, good job," Mr. Sean said, patting my shoulder awkwardly with a rough hand covered in beach sand. It was so out of character for him.

Jewel whirled around and gave me a big hug, attempting to keep her soiled hands off my back. She took a shaky breath, and we just sat for a moment, holding one another. I watched over her shoulder as Finn wrapped a jacket around Moz's leg. Moz wriggled around as he tied it tightly.

"Is he alright?" Mr. Sean asked as Jewel released me.

"Hey, you think I'll get a cool scar out of this?" Moz asked as Darren helped him sit up.

I released a tense sigh and gave a relieved chuckle. "He's fine."

Finn helped Jewel up and walked her to the

water to rise her hands clean. I watched how sweet he was to her. How he watched over her.

"I think you should all buy me dinner now. I mean, I almost died and all," Moz noted.

"You are so dramatic!" Darren scoffed.

"I was poisoned!" Moz defended. "You don't know what it was like! My whole life fluttered before my eyes."

"Okay, remind me, why did we save your wings again?" Darren mocked, shaking his head and helping Moz to his feet.

Moz gawked. "Seriously, I done could have bleeded out to dead!"

"*Bled* to *death*? From that little scratch?" Darren bantered. The two began heading slowly back inland. "Let's go clean up your boo-boo and get you a band-aid. And maybe some grammar."

A searing pain stabbed at my head and ears one last time. I fought to stay upright.

"I will have you. Yes, you have proven that you will make a fine wife. You will see just how much better you will be by my side. I'll see you soon, my darling," sneered Byrein's unmistakable voice.

And just like that, it was gone.

"Esmari?" Mr. Sean pressed.

"Byrein," I told him.

Footsteps in the sand crunched near where we stood, and I didn't dare speak more of it. I glanced up as Jewel and Finn strode past us. Jewel was back to her chipper self, seemingly unfazed by the events we had all just encountered. She turned to me as she passed.

"Are you coming?" Jewel asked.

I flicked a look at Finn. His gaze fell on the back of Jewel with kindness. I couldn't help but notice his longing for another moment with her.

Looking back at Jewel, I smiled. "I'll catch up with you in a moment."

"Okay! Don't be long. Be safe please!" she noted, waving as she turned back around.

When they were a few strides away, I turned back to Mr. Sean, who was still waiting on an explanation. I took a deep breath, but it was Mr. Sean who spoke.

"Byrein wants you."

"He wants me to be his—" I hesitated. The very thought was sickening.

"His wife," Mr. Sean stated plainly.

He knew all this time?

In this world, people are naturally driven by power. I thought that it was what set a Royal apart from others. While that is part of it, it doesn't define who you are and who you are meant to be. So, many are not satisfied with the power they have. They endlessly seek out to have more. I was so afraid of becoming one of these people that I found myself shying away from what my true potential could be.

That is, until that day on the beach.

The day I discovered what I could do, and, more importantly, what I was strong enough not to do. Holding someone else's power in my hands made one thing very clear: I am no longer afraid of this power I have inside of me.

www.ingramcontent.com/pod-product-compliance
Lightning Source LLC
Chambersburg PA
CBHW061615190726

48288CB00007B/2325